Fifty-six-year-old George Reynolds lies critically ill in hospital after crashing his car on the way back from an RAF reunion in September 1978. But a man looking exactly like Mr Reynolds is being held as a suspected Nazi spy in a remote wartime RAF guardroom. And he has some very awkward questions to answer.

Other questions need answering:

Why did retired Wing Commander Clive Prescott take up residence at Lynton Down in 1973 at the request of psychic researcher, Dorothy Beresford?

What do the villagers of Lynton Down know about the so-called *phantom squadron*?

Why has the wing commander persuaded the prickly Lord Redford to call a meeting of all the villagers exactly 38 years after the Battle of Britain?

Does it have something to do with helping the ghostly airmen who haunt the village and the old airfield? And what part can George Reynolds play in order to prevent them becoming malignant?

This masterly tale of the supernatural is guaranteed to thrill the senses whenever it's not chilling the blood.

GW00692309

To my wife Vicki, who wanted a ghost story.

# HELP US TO DIE

## BARRIE COOKE

JANUS PUBLISHING COMPANY
London, England

First published in Great Britain 1993
by Janus Publishing Company

Copyright © Barrie Cooke 1993

**British Library Cataloguing-in-Publication Data.**
**A catalogue record for this book is available from the British**
**Library.**

ISBN 1 85756 018 3

Cover design David Murphy

Printed and bound in Great Britain by
Antony Rowe Ltd, Chippenham, Wiltshire

# Chapter 1

The little green mini sped along the narrow country lane; its headlights, faithfully following the car's erratic course, swept the rain spattered road ahead, lighting up the grass verges and hedgerows, first on one side, and then the other.

Behind the wheel, George Reynolds licked his dry lips distastefully and squinted through the waterlogged windscreen. The dull throb behind his eyes foretold the beginnings of a hangover. He was drunk – he knew that – he shouldn't have had that last double scotch: fatal. But, what the hell, it was only once in a while and George had attended every squadron reunion since he had been demobbed in 1946. Mind you, he mused regretfully, there weren't many of the old crowd left now. For many years, whilst the squadron was still operational, each reunion had been revitalised with an injection of new blood, but since it had been disbanded, their numbers had decreased appreciably. George himself didn't know how much longer he could go on attending these functions. He was 56 now and the journey from Saltdean to London was becoming more arduous on each occasion; but what the hell, he thought again, I guess I'm good for another couple more yet. He relaxed and let his mind wander over the events of a happy, nostalgic evening.

Twin lights suddenly loomed up out of a bend in the road ahead and sped towards him on a collision course. Blinded by the glare, he barely had time to yank the wheel around before the advancing vehicle, its horn blaring, swept past, drenching the little car in a welter of spray and mud. Before his eyes had time to adjust to the sudden darkness, the bend in the road was upon him. The bank rushed to meet him and, in that split second, he knew he wasn't going to make it. Stamping on the brakes, he hauled the wheel around in a desperate attempt to avoid the inevitable collision. The tyres screeched protestingly as, wheels locked, they aquaplaned over the wet road surface. He felt the back begin to swing and the solid jar as the rear nearside wheel hit the sloping bank. The car tilted and span across the road to the accompaniment of shattering glass and the grinding of distorting metal. It mounted the bank on the opposite side of the road, teetered, then slowly rolled back, coming to rest on its roof with a final thud.

The headlights, still operational, lit the scene of the accident with a ghostly radiance, the twin beams, directed upwards at a shallow angle, converging on the line of trees bordering the top of the bank. In the unnatural silence that followed, the only sounds were the soft whirr of the wheels as they span on their axle shafts, the spattering of rain and the mournful soughing of the wind through the trees. Soon, the wheels ceased to turn, the rain stopped and only the dark rustle of the wind prevailed.

George Reynolds wanted to wake up. He struggled to open his eyes but they were attached to leaden weights and the result was a barely preceptible flicker. He was sinking into a deep, dark pit at the bottom of which was eternal oblivion and, with this realisation, he made a supreme effort. His arms and legs twitched convulsively and his head rolled from side to side. Suddenly, his eyes opened wide and he was staring at the stars through a delicate latticework of branches, fitfully waving in the night breeze.

For a while he just lay there gazing uncomprehendingly at the flickering stars, and wondering, in a detached manner why he wasn't looking at his own bedroom ceiling. He moved his head and his eyes rested on the upturned car. He saw the corner, felt the violent lurch – disorientation, confusion, pain – heard the shattering of glass, then darkness, total and complete. 'Oh my God.' He leapt to his feet – it was a reflex action and quite involuntary – and scrambled down the bank. The car was a write-off; he could see that at a glance. The framework was twisted and the front crushed in. The engine had been forced back through the bulkhead and was protruding into the driving compartment. The steering wheel had snapped and the rim was hanging crazily over the column. There was glass everywhere.

He gazed at the wreckage and span a front wheel dejectedly. 'Sorry, old girl,' he muttered, 'all my fault.' Hell, what a mess and what a fool he'd been. What was he going to do now? It was only then, and with mounting fear, that he thought of himself. He hurried around to the front of the car and stood in front of the headlights. First he inspected his hands and arms; no blood and, as far as he could tell, nothing broken. He felt his ribs and stomach; no pain, everything OK there. He flexed his legs and feet; again no pain and nothing broken. Almost fearfully, he put his hands to his face, felt his nose, eyes, ears, ran his hands through his hair and then looked at them in the headlights. No blood, nothing. It was impossible, he wasn't even bruised. He had heard of drunks surviving falls which would have crippled more sober men – something to do with them being more relaxed – but this was ridiculous! How could he possibly have survived that battering, much less walk away from it unscathed?

He frowned, concentrating his mind once more on those frightful few seconds. Yes, he'd felt pain, he was certain of that, but there was no pain now, so why not? He looked at the door, torn from one hinge and sagging open. He thought, 'I must have gone through there,' and with that thought came a great joy and profound relief. He was not a very religious man, but now he fell on his knees and gave thanks to Almighty God for his deliverance.

Now the problem arose as to how he could get help. Should he stay with the car on the remote chance that someone would happen along, or start hoofing it in the hope that he would find an AA box or a house with a telephone? He glanced at his watch. It was 2.30 a.m. Laura, his wife, would be frantic. That decided him, he must get to a telephone. He gave the car a last affectionate pat and set off into the darkness. And thus he never saw the pitiful, twisted and bloodied bundle that lay huddled only a few feet away, on the very spot where he regained consciousness.

7

# Chapter 2

George walked about a quarter of a mile when a branch of the road opened up to the left, forming a 'T' junction. He paused, listening. Voices came to him faintly from the side road and, peering into the gloom, he thought he could discern lights appearing and disappearing among the trees. His luck still held, then. There were people up there and that meant help. He began walking towards the lights but, after a few yards, his pace slowed and he stopped, his eyes straining the darkness ahead, his head cocked to one side, listening.

The disembodied voices seemed to be all around, but were too low to form intelligible speech. The brief sentences, spoken sotto voce, sometimes close at hand, sometimes further away, coupled with the eerie flickering and bobbing of lights, like fireflies in the bushes on a summer's evening, spoke of a party of men searching the woods. What were they searching for? And at this time in the morning? Some sixth sense counselled caution and suddenly George felt very naked standing in the middle of the road. If there was dirty work afoot, he wanted no part of it; he was in enough trouble already. Swiftly and silently he crossed to a ditch running alongside the road, scrambled down its shallow bank, and lay there, listening.

The sounds of the search grew nearer. In the still night air, he could hear the occasional sharp crack of a twig and the rustle of feet moving through the leaves. From time to time, there came a metallic clicking, usually followed by a muffled oath of annoyance. Whoever they were, they were obviously trying to be as quiet as possible, but a wood, especially at night, is not the best place in the world to proceed silently.

Suddenly, a voice directly above his head hurled a stage

whisper into the night. 'Clark, you bloody fool, keep that bleedin' light shrouded. Do you want him to spot us?' There was a muffled apology from Clark, and the search continued apace.

How long George lay there, he would never know, but it was long enough for the cold night air to penetrate his bones and a cramp to attack his right leg. Flexing his foot and gritting his teeth against the pain, he waited until the sounds of the search melted into the distance, then crawled painfully out of the ditch. He stamped his foot and rubbed the knotted calf muscle until returning circulation brought a blessed relief.

He sighed, straightened up and felt a cold, round circle of steel press into his neck. His heart gave a lurch and his scalp prickled. He made an involuntary movement and the ring of steel dug deeper into his neck.

'Don't try it pal. This 'ere's a .303 pokin' into the back of yer neck, an' if yer try anything funny, I'll spatter yer brains all over the road. Nah, turn around slowly an' let's 'ave a look at yer.'

Frightened and bewildered, George did as he was told and a strong light shone directly into his face, blinding him. His captor was just a vague shadow in the blackness beyond the light, but the tip of the .303 Enfield rifle, only an inch away from his chest, was real enough.

'Look,' he began, 'I don't know who you are, but there's obviously been . . .'

'Shuddup an' keep quiet.' His captor's voice rose to an excited shout. Sergeant Hawkins, I've got him sarge. Over here, near the 'T' junction.'

'Good lad, hold him there, I'm coming.' The voice came from somewhere up the road and was immediately followed by the patter of running feet. A moment later Sergeant Hawkins arrived, accompanied, as far as George could tell, by another two men. Strong hands grabbed his shoulder and he was pulled around to be subjected to another torch scrutiny.

'I was sittin' on the bank up there sarge,' said George's captor, puffed up with pride at his achievement, 'when 'e pops up under my feet, so to speak.' He giggled at his little joke. 'Don't know who was more surprised, 'im or me.'

'All right, lad, you did a good job; now, cut along and round up the others.' The rifle was withdrawn, to be replaced by the snub nose of a Sten gun.

'You,' the Sten poked him in the ribs, 'put your hands behind your back.'

Dumbly, George did as he was told and a pair of handcuffs were snapped over his wrists. 'Now, walk,' and he was given a shove from behind.

After his initial protest, George had remained meekly silent and compliant, frightened of the consequences, but handcuffing him was the last straw. Who the hell did these guys think they were, anyway? Damned officious bastards. Anger overcame prudence and he swung round on the sergeant.

'Now, look here, Sergeant, you'd better have a bloody good reason for subjecting me to these outrages, because if you haven't God help you. I gather I've strayed into some sensitive MOD establishment, but surely you must realise it's all a mistake. I had an accident just down the road and I was looking for help.'

The Sten prodded him again, this time in the pit of his stomach, making him gasp with pain. 'You can save your breath until we get back to the guardroom, then you are welcome to sing your little heart out. Now, **move**.'

He was forcibly turned around and propelled up the road. Two vague shapes fell in either side of him and, seeing the futility of further argument, he did as he was told.

After about a quarter of a mile, the road ran into a red and white striped pole barrier with a circular disc in the centre inscribed with the word *HALT*. To the left of the barrier, an armed guard stood at ease outside a sentry box. As the party approached, he sprang to attention and issued a challenge. 'Halt. Who goes there?'

'Friend, search party. Sergeant Hawkins i/c.'

'Advance, friend and be recognised.'

'Hold him.' George felt his arms firmly grasped by his escort while Sergeant Hawkins stepped up to the guard. He produced an identity card which the sentry examined by shielded torchlight. He shone the torch momentarily on the Sergeant's face, returned his identity card and raised the barrier.

'Pass, friend.'

The situation became more ludicrous by the moment. If this was a restricted zone, then where were the warning notices? and why was the place in darkness? Not a gleam of light showed anywhere. And another thing; that ridiculous form of challenge – it had gone out with the ark. George was no longer angry; he began to feel uneasy. There was something very wrong here.

They passed under the barrier and skirted a neatly trimmed grass verge protected by a low, whitewashed chain fence. The scent of flowers hung heavily on the late summer air, while, from a long, single-storied wooden building came the faint sound of music.

It was towards this building that George was propelled, pushed up three steps then halted on the verandah before a door bearing the title *GUARDROOM*. To the right of the door, a full length mirror was affixed to the wall which George recognised as being statutory to all service establishments. In its reflection, servicemen and women were supposed to add those final touches to their appearance before launching themselves on an unsuspecting public.

George glanced into the mirror and froze. Only his own reflection stared back at him. Of his escort, there was no sign. Before he had time to recover from the shock, he was ushered into a confined space between two doors. Sergeant Hawkins closed the other then, after a moment of claustrophobic darkness, the inner one opened and George was shoved roughly into a brightly lit room.

Blinking in the strong light, George found himself standing before a semi-circular counter, topped with highly polished brown lino. The room beyond was a typical service guardroom, the parquet floor polished to perfection, the brass and chrome work gleaming. Shields and trophies stood resplendent in a glass cabinet against the wall, to the right, either side of which were doors, one barred and labelled *CELLS*, the other *ABLUTIONS*. A board of keys stood near a heavily curtained window above which hung a calendar. A radio rested on a shelf, while from a gramophone came the strains of Glen Miller's *Moonlight Serenade*. George's attention was drawn to three posters on the opposite wall; one showed the ranks and badges of the Royal Air Force; another headed *KNOW THE ENEMY* showed various Luftwaffe aircraft in silhouette, all of World War 2 vintage. The third poster showed two soldiers standing at a bar, deep in conversation while, standing close by, a sinister figure listened intently. Underneath were the words *CARELESS TALK COSTS LIVES*.

There were three other airmen in the room; one, a corporal, lounged in a leather chair, reading *The Wizard*, while the other two were playing cards on a table, upon which stood two chipped, brown tin mugs containing steaming hot cocoa.

George's two escorts left him and proceeded to help themselves to cocoa from an urn standing on a wooden bench. Sergeant Hawkins shoved George around the counter and into the centre of the room.

'Pour me out one too, Taylor,' he said, as he reached for the telephone.

The two airmen had stopped playing cards, the corporal had put down his *Wizard* and all three were staring at George, hostility reflected in their faces. George tried to ignore them and devoted his attention to a situation that had all the ingredients of a nightmare. Those uniforms they were wearing were the old blue serge jackets and trousers that hadn't been general issue for years; and those posters? He remembered them from the war years. He began to feel frightened; not the kind of fear he had experienced after the accident – things had seemed normal, then. No, this was a mind-numbing fear of the unknown. His chest tightened and his hands grew clammy with sweat. He was dimly aware that Sergeant Hawkins was speaking into the telephone.

'Yes, sir, an intruder. We received word that a parachute was seen to fall in the vicinity. I organised a search party and we spotted this chap crawling out of a ditch near the camp. I thought you might like a word with him.' He shot George an appraising glance. 'Fiftyish I'd say, sir; light brown sports jacket, grey flannel trousers, no turn ups and – just a moment, sir.' He put down the receiver and pulled George towards him,

12

examining the badge he wore on his lapel. He gave George an astonished look and returned to the phone. 'The cheeky blighter's wearing a 54 Squadron badge,' he said, incredulously. He listened for a moment, then said, 'Right sir,' and replaced the receiver.

George was vaguely aware that the sergeant was speaking to him. His mouth was forming words but they were a confused and incoherent jumble. His attention was riveted on the sergeant's eyes. They were the eyes of a blind man, staring blankly out of deep sockets, the irises pale, the pupils white and translucent. Looking at the others, George realised with a shock that they too had the same defect. Sightless eyes stared at him from all directions.

His face was grasped by a strong hand and his head shaken violently from side to side.

'Mister, I'm talking to you.'

George swallowed hard and fought to control his shaking limbs. 'God, I mustn't let them see I'm frightened.' He forced himself to look into the sergeant's face.

'Sorry,' he mumbled, 'I'm a little shaken up – the accident and all that. What was it you were saying?'

'I was saying it's a night in the cells for you, my lad. The Station Admin. Officer, Squadron Leader Jenkins will see you in the morning, eight o'clock sharp.'

Sergeant Hawkins placed his Sten on the counter and sipped his cocoa with relish. He was a burly fellow, probably in his mid-thirties, and looked the picture of fitness. George quickly put away any thought of escape.

'May I have a cup of that cocoa?' he asked, meekly.

'Billings, a cup of your best cocoa for the gentleman.'

Billings, one of George's escort, grinned at the sergeant's elaborate courtesy and proceeded to do his bidding.

The cocoa was hot and sweet and, as he sipped it, he felt a new strength, accompanied by a partial return of his natural optimism. He began to assess the situation. He was being held at an RAF station – which one, he had no idea – and that knowledge gave him a certain amount of comfort. He had been associated with the RAF for most of his life; ever since he volunteered for the service in May 1940. He'd served throughout the war as an armourer and was demobbed in June 1946. In 1958, he joined the Air Training Corps as a civilian instructor and was commissioned in the RAFVR Training Branch in 1965. Since then, as a flight lieutenant, he had commanded three squadrons and had recently been elevated to the rank of squadron leader and given a post as a wing staff officer. He had attended summer camps for many years, the last being at RAF Scampton only a few weeks ago. He had many influential friends in the service so, in all the circumstances, he felt no apprehension concerning his forthcoming interview with Sqn. Ldr. Jenkins.

No, that wasn't what was troubling him. There was something else, something unnatural. Apart from their eyes, there was an alien quality about these people – about the whole set-up – which made his flesh creep. Why, for God's sake, had he not been able to see the reflections of his escort in the mirror? He shuddered at the recollection.

There was something else bugging him, too, nagging at the back of his mind, clamouring to be let out. It was the key, the answer to everything. Was it something he had seen? something they'd said? The clues were all there, but he just couldn't put the pieces together.

Sgt. Hawkins drained his cup and wiped his lips with the back of his hand. 'Billings,' he picked up the Sten and threw it at him. 'Empty that and stick it back in the rack. And now, sir,' he confronted George who wondered whether the respectful 'sir' was genuine or mockery. 'Your name, please.'

'George Reynolds,' he replied, shortly. It was just about the only piece of information he was ready to volunteer to this chap tonight. The sergeant produced a memo pad, licked a pencil and wrote down, *George Reynolds*.

'Where do you come from?'

George saw no reason why he should withhold that information.

'Saltdean. It's near Brighton,' he added, helpfully.

'I know where it is,' snapped the sergeant. He made another entry in his memo pad.

'Empty your pockets.'

14

George turned his back on the sergeant and wriggled his manacled hands. 'Delighted,' he said affably, 'but as you can see, at the moment my hands are tied.'

Sgt. Hawkins grinned. 'The man has a sense of humour,' he commented to the room at large. He produced a key, unlocked the cuffs and placed them on a shelf under the counter.

George flexed his fingers and massaged his wrists before divesting his pockets of their contents. He carried very little on his person. There was a handkerchief emblazoned with his initials, a comb, a ballpoint pen, which the sergeant examined curiously, his RAFVR identity card and a wallet, which was the last item to be inspected. As he opened it, Sgt. Hawkins gave a low whistle of surprise, extracted the banknotes and spread them out on the counter. There were a fiver and three one pound notes; each note was subjected to a keen scrutiny, which included holding them up to the light. When he had finished, Sgt. Hawkins replaced them on the counter.

'Come over here, lads.' The airmen dutifully crowded around him.

'Ever seen anything like these before?'

'Looks like banknotes,' said the corporal.

Sgt. Hawkins gave a gasp of exasperation. 'Thank you, Cpl. Phillips.' His voice was heavy with sarcasm. 'Without that little pearl of wisdom, I might never have known. Of course they're banknotes, you idiot, but what sort of banknotes, that's what I want to know?'

'There's nothing strange about them, Sgt. Hawkins,' said George, wondering what all the fuss was about. 'I can assure you, they're perfectly genuine.'

'Perfectly genuine? Who are you trying to kid, mister.' Sgt. Hawkins pulled out his own wallet, extracted a pound note and shoved it under George's nose. 'There,' he said, triumphantly, 'that's a genuine pound note.'

George looked at the note and his heart missed a beat. It was of the type in circulation for many years before they started changing the design and size. All at once, he knew what had been worrying him all along. He glanced once more at the calendar and all the pieces fell into place. It was dated 1940.

# Chapter 3

The month was right and that was all he had noticed during that first quick glance, but the day and year must have registered subconsciously and that was the key that unlocked the puzzle.

Now he knew the reason for that archaic challenge, the old fashioned uniforms, his arrest as a suspected parachutist and an RAF station cloaked in darkness. The station was on a wartime footing at the height of the Battle of Britain!

Unable to accept, even then, the implications of his discovery, he briefly toyed with the idea that he had stumbled onto a film set, but his peremptory arrest, the missing reflections and those ghastly white eyes finally convinced him. Now he knew what they were and the knowledge brought with it a wave of terror. They were ghosts. Somewhere in the heart of the Sussex downs there was a ghost station reliving those momentous events of 1940, treading predestined paths, perhaps for all eternity.

But where did he, George Reynolds, who was a mere 18 in 1940, fit into this picture? Surely his presence would be a disturbing influence on that ghostly, rhythmic cycle. And why did they appear so real, so substantial? Ghosts were supposed to be nebulous wraiths, transparent and untouchable. But apart from the two anomalies already noted, these people appeared to be perfectly normal beings. Additionally, and here his heart skipped a beat, he was being accepted as one of them. Why, oh dear God, why?

His legs suddenly refused to take his weight, his knees shook and he clutched at the counter for support.

'May I sit down?' he asked, weakly.

The sergeant studied him unsympathetically. 'Get him a chair, somebody.'

A chair, one of the wooden, folding sort, much loved of the service, was placed beside him and he sank into it, thankfully. After a little while, his heart ceased to beat painfully against his ribs and his brain cleared sufficiently to allow him logical thought. Those notes were going to be difficult to explain, not to mention the coins which Sgt. Hawkins hadn't yet got around to examining. He needed time to think. A night in the cells is what the sergeant had said. Perhaps if he clammed up and refused to talk to anyone except Sqn. Ldr. Jenkins, Sergeant Hawkins would see the futility of questioning him further and lock him up for the night. George eyed the sergeant critically. He didn't look like one who would give up that easily but, right now, it was all he could think of and any plan was better than none at all. Having come to that decision, he felt much better and waited stoically for the sergeant to make his next move. He hadn't long to wait.

'Now, mister, let's have the truth, shall we?' Sgt. Hawkins leaned on the counter and tapped the notes. The 'sightless' eyes stared at him, unfocused and, seemingly unseeing. 'Where did you get these notes?'

George folded his arms and stared back defiantly. 'I refuse to answer any more of your questions. I'll sing my heart out, as you so delightfully put it, only to the squadron leader.'

Sgt. Hawkins straightened up slowly, then his hand flashed out catching George a blow on the cheek that knocked his head sideways.

'Atta boy, sarge,' yelled Cpl. Phillips, sensing blood. 'Duff 'im up, Nazi bastard.'

'Wind your neck in, corporal.' He resumed his nonchalant stance at the counter.

'That, mister was just a sample. This little chat can be either pleasant or painful; it's entirely up to you.'       .

But George wasn't listening. He was wondering why the hell that slap didn't hurt any more. He had felt the first vicious sting, then nothing. There had been no gradual diminishment

17

of pain; just a sudden cessation and, as George found out when he touched his cheek, no consequent numbness.

Sgt. Hawkins sighed, misinterpreting George's bewilderment for stubbornness.

'I can see we're going to have to do this the hard way.' He heaved himself off the counter just as the telephone rang. He turned and picked up the receiver.

'Guardroom, Sar'nt Hawkins.' He listened for a moment, then said, 'Right,' and replaced the receiver.

'Air raid message Yellow, lads,' he said, briskly, '72 plus bandits approaching our sector.' He plucked his gas mask and steel helmet off a hook on the wall and issued a stream of orders.

'Taylor, stand by the alarm button. Cpl. Phillips, get on the phone and warn the village police. The rest of you, grab your kit and get down the shelter, pronto.'

As the airmen leapt about to do his bidding, he grabbed George by the arm. 'Come on, chum, I'm not taking any chances with you.' He selected a bunch of keys from a key board and, still holding George's arm, unlocked the door leading to the cells. He pushed George into the corridor and opened the first cell on the right. 'Inside!' He gave George a shove, then closed and locked the cell door. Before departing, he scowled at George through the bars. 'You're a lucky man. Your friends arrived just in time.' George heard the outer door close and the key grate in the lock, then there was silence.

George looked around his cell. It was lit by a single blue night-light glowing centrally above the door. The walls were whitewashed brick and an iron bed stood in one corner, complete with three straw-filled 'biscuits'; a sausage-shaped pillow, also straw-filled, and four neatly folded blankets. Under the bed was a yellow tin box with a hinged lid. George hadn't seen one of those since his square-bashing days. In it each recruit put all his possessions which were not part of his service issue, those things which were not considered fit for the service-orientated eyes of the inspecting officer. There was a small shelf above the bed on which one kept his No. 1 uniform and great-coat, the trousers at the bottom, neatly folded into four razor

18

sharp creases, the jacket on top, folded to the same length with the belt to the front and, topping the lot, the greatcoat, sometimes packed with cardboard to make it square, with two highly polished buttons gleaming centrally. The only other furniture in the room was a windsor chair and a small wooden locker.

George spread the biscuits over the bed and laid on them, resting his head on the blankets. The sergeant was right; the air raid had indeed come at a most propitious moment. He had needed time to think and now, in the quiet of his cell, he began to retrace the events of the past hour or so, trying to find some logical explanation that would account for finding himself in this ghastly situation.

'Ghastly?' he thought, 'Huh, ghostly more like.' Hells bells, how could there be a logical explanation for something so illogical? He gave it up and concentrated on the money problem. Somehow he had to find a satisfactory explanation for possessing Queen Elizabeth II decimal currency in 1940. Ye gods, the mind boggled. But boggled though the mind might be, he had to find one, and his brow creased with the effort of concentration.

The undulating wail of a siren interrupted his thoughts and, as he listened, he remembered those far off wartime days when that selfsame sound brought to the young George Reynolds a thrill of excitement, tinged with fear.

He saw, once more, the bulbous barrage balloons suspended motionless and silver against the blue summer sky, now criss-crossed with the white contrails of fighters dancing a deadly ballet to the accompaniment of the staccato stammer of machine guns. He heard again the vibrating drone of the airborne armada, spreading over the horizon and darkening the sky with their numbers. Heard the hollow bangs of the anti-aircraft guns, to be followed moments later by the crump of exploding shells; the sudden 'whoosh' and concussion of a bomb exploding nearby, the frantic clanging of bells as fire engines sped through the stricken city.

Suddenly, he sat bolt upright, his head cocked to one side, listening. That all too familiar drone wasn't part of his reverie,

19

neither were the distant crackle of exploding anti-aircraft shells. The drone grew louder and now he could distinguish the higher pitched whine of the night fighters and the sporadic splutter of machine guns.

As the host passed overhead, the night was filled with the shattering roar of their engines as they strained to reach their target before the fuel gauges warned the crew that they had reached the point of no return.

The building shook and so did George, and it wasn't entirely due to the vibration. That locked door and the small confines of the cell were giving him a nasty bout of claustrophobia. His mouth grew dry and his palms damp as his mind filled with the nightmare picture of a sky, raining bombs, each one destined to explode on or around his little cell. Lying prone on the bed, his hands clenched tightly around the curve of the bedrail, he waited and sweated in an agony of anticipation for that high-pitched scream which would herald the release of the first stick of bombs. But it never came. Instead, a new sound was born out of a long burst of machine gun fire. It began with a zoom and gradually developed into the tortured scream of engines being pushed to their limit. The sound continued for some time, growing louder by the second, until it abruptly terminated in a shattering explosion and the ground shook. Bombers and fighters continued on their way, the throb of their engines fading into the distance until they could no longer be heard; and an unnatural silence, heavy and oppressive, took their place – a silence in which George clearly heard the beat of his heart and the rushing of blood in his temples. Gradually his heart settled down to normal rhythm and he passed the back of his hand over his clammy brow and wiped his palms on the 'biscuits'.

Fear gave way to rage and he cursed Sgt. Hawkins to hell and back again for shutting him up alone in this cell. 'God, I'll have something to say to that bastard when I see him,' he muttered through clenched teeth.

He heaved himself into a sitting position and then froze. A tiny circle of yellow light was burning itself into the cell door. This was quickly surrounded by a shimmering, shapeless glow, its edges tinged with blue. George's eyes widened in horror and his muscles locked in fear as he watched the glow expand and assume a vaguely human form. It detached itself from the door and entered the cell, floating towards his bed, swaying as it approached, the radiance of the shimmering form and the little circle of yellow light illuminating the cell walls with a cold, ghostly light.

It paused, its shape flickering. Suddenly, the light grew brighter and in that instant George's muscles responded to the frantic signals from his brain. He leapt off the bed, flattened himself against the wall and his mouth opened in a long, high-pitched scream.

# Chapter 4

Old Sam Bassett was in his element. He had just successfully tickled his sixth trout out of the river and into the large canvas haversack he wore slung round his shoulder, and he whistled silently through his teeth as he made his way through the wedge of trees that bordered the old airfield.

It wasn't so much the amount of trout that he had filtched from Lord Redford's river that produced so blithe a whistle; it was the thought that he had done so, once again, right under the nose of his Lordship's gamekeeper, Ralph Morgan.

Dark though it was, Sam stepped sure-footedly along one of the many paths that ran through the wood. He knew those woods as he knew the inside of his own house and he was equally at home in them. Born and bred in the nearby village, he was one of nature's children and had spent a lifetime roaming the fields and woods, poaching a little here, scrumping a little there, until he knew every stream, pathway and hillock within a radius of 10 miles; and it was this superior knowledge that had, so far, kept him out of Ralph Morgan's clutches.

Old Sam was the bane of Ralph's life and he (Ralph) would cheerfully have given a month's salary to catch him in the act, but the old devil was too slippery and knew the area too well. Many had been the time he had spotted him through his binoculars, up to his old tricks, and on these occasions, his heart pounding exultantly, he would worm his way silently towards his victim, scratching his hands and face on brambles, getting soaked to the skin crossing intervening streams and crawling over the occasional cowpat, until, at last, with a cry of, 'Got you, you old bastard,' he would leap out of a covering bush, only to find old Sam was no longer there. Then, bedraggled and dishevelled, tired and frustrated, he would head for home, shaking his fist at the sky and swearing a great oath that, if it took him the rest of his natural life, he would, one day, have the infinite pleasure of putting old Sam behind bars.

This, then, was Ralph's dream, and to this end, he had decided to revise his tactics. He had given up trying to defeat old Sam at his own game and decided to employ a little applied psychology.

A wall, 10 feet high, capped with glass shards embedded in concrete, bounded the estate and, in the whole of the five miles perimeter, there were only five gaps – five points at which old Sam could enter or leave the estate. The largest of these gaps permitted access from the A23 to the side road leading to the main gate of the old airfield, and was used now solely for the purpose of transporting farm produce to market. Of the other four, he could immediately rule out one. This was the entrance to the Hall itself, and was closed by a beautiful pair of wrought iron gates, each one emblazoned with the Redford family crest. Through these gates ran the winding, poplar-lined drive that led to the porticoed entrance of Holstead Hall, a rambling six-teenth century building, which had been a gift to the Redford family from a grateful Charles II. Not even old Sam would dare enter by that route.

Another gap had been caused when a lorry burst its tyre and buried its bonnet in the wall amid an avalanche of bricks and mortar. This had happened two years ago, and although Ralph had made frequent representations to his lordship, it was still unrepaired and only a few strands of rusty barbed wire bridged the gaping hole. Certainly that would prove no obstacle to old Sam.

The river running through the estate afforded the only other two entry and exit points. This was where it flowed under the road on entering and leaving the estate, and it would be the easiest thing in the world for old Sam to scramble down the bank and wade through the shallow water as it passed under the bridge.

So, Ralph reasoned, if I can't catch the old rascal on the

23

estate, I'll nab him as he leaves, and he immediately began a random watch on all the escape points.

Now, this was a very hit-and-miss affair as Ralph well knew. Old Sam was much too cunning to make regular forages into the estate and Ralph calculated that, when he did, he always varied his entry and exit points; therefore it would have to be pure luck which placed Ralph at the right spot, at the right time and on the right night to catch old Sam. Nevertheless, he was determined to try.

Right now, he was beginning to doubt the wisdom of that course of action. Perhaps it would be better if he just stuck to one location. It was rather like filling in a pools coupon; some people preferred to vary their numbers each week, others kept to one set, hoping one day to hit the jackpot.

Tonight, Ralph had chosen to watch the airfield entrance and now, as he sat on the crumbling steps of the old guardroom verandah, his 12-bore shotgun straddling his knees, he gazed at the low, two-storeyed, flat-roofed building across the road. This was the old station headquarters, still wearing its wartime coat of camouflage, its broken windows, flaking paint and the crumbling pillars of its main entrance proclaiming its dereliction.

In his mind's eye, he pictured the airfield as it was in its heyday, its bustling roads filled with servicemen and women and transports of every shape and size. Bulbous bowsers hastening to refuel the thirsty aircraft, its hangars echoing to the humming of servicing trolleys, the yammering of compressor engines and the hammering of aircraft panels being beaten back into shape. The rattling of ammunition belts as the armourers fed them from the tanks and into the Browning machine guns. Pilots relaxing around the dispersal hut, tradesmen scattered around the parked aircraft, kicking a makeshift ball about or, maybe, leaning against a wheel chock, writing a letter home; all ready to leap into action the moment the strident clamour of the external telephone bell announced a scramble. Ralph sighed, remembering the days when he, too, had been a part of that scene.

Something he saw out of the corner of his eye attracted his attention and he glanced sharply in the direction of the access road. Out of the darkness, a tiny pin point of light had suddenly materialised, expanding as it approached into a shimmering blue glow. It paused for a while at the airfield entrance then continued its advance, slowly resolving into four wispy, insubstantial figures. He blinked and rubbed his eyes. He was tired, God knows he was tired, and tired people sometimes see strange things, especially at night with only the faint luminescence of the stars to alleviate the otherwise total darkness. He looked again, and this time there was no doubt about it. They were there all right, and heading straight for him. A cold shiver ran up his spine and his hair bristled.

He had heard rumours that the old airfield was haunted, and some simple folk swore that certain buildings in the village were also haunted, particularly the local pub; but Ralph, being a down to earth sort of chap, had always pooh-poohed the idea. But now he was seeing it for himself and, for a split second, he sat glued to the spot, his eyes bulging, watching with awful fascination, the four spectral figures gliding silently towards him. Then, suddenly, the strength flowed back into his limbs and, with a low, shuddering moan he leapt to his feet. His torch and shotgun clattered to the ground and he ran.

And how he ran! His feet hardly touched the ground as he strove to put as much distance as possible between himself and those ghostly figures. He ran until he staggered with fatigue and his heart was fit to burst. He became dimly aware that his feet no longer scrunched on gravel, that he had left the road and was now running on grass.

With that knowledge, the reserves of strength he had been drawing on for the last quarter mile, ran out. He stumbled and fell heavily onto the cool, damp grass and lay there, his chest heaving and sucking painful gulps of air into his craving lungs. How long he lay there he would never know, but when his heart had settled down to a more or less normal rhythm and his breathing had become deeper and less irregular, he rolled onto his back and gazed up at the star-speckled sky.

What on earth was it he had seen? That those wispy figures had been ghosts he had no doubt. No more would he ridicule those villagers who swopped tales of their encounters with the supernatural over a pint at the local. Ye gods, no; he would be among the foremost of them, expounding his experiences as eagerly as the next. He struggled into a sitting position and looked about him nervously.

No blue glow or ghostly apparitions pursued him; he was alone in a wilderness of darkness and he cast about him in an endeavour to fix his position. Just ahead, in the direction from whence he had come, loomed two dark masses which he was able to identify as two of the four airfield hangars. To his left, in front of the farther hangar, he was able to make out the shape of the control tower silhouetted against the starry backdrop. So, his headlong flight had taken him roughly 20 yards past the pitted, weed-strewn peritrack onto the airfield proper, which meant that he had run, flat out, for close on three-quarters of a mile. He rose shakily to his feet, mildly surprised at having run that distance at his age. He must be fitter than he'd thought, but then, it was amazing to what lengths the body could be pushed, once the adrenalin started to flow.

He stood for a while, breathing in the cool night air, waiting for the shaking spasms to cease. The old airfield, at which he had felt so much at home, had now become a place of horror where, behind every bush and shadow, there lurked a hidden menace. With a final shudder, he turned his back on the station and set off across the airfield.

He had only walked a few steps, when he suddenly stopped and turned again. His shotgun, where was his shotgun? He quickly returned to the spot where he had collapsed and, falling on his knees, began a blind search of the area, exploring every inch with his hands. It wasn't there. Hell, where was it? Lord Redford would crucify him if he lost it. It was his lordships favourite weapon and he had only lent it to Ralph because Ralph's shotgun had a broken hammer catch. He had pleaded with his lordship to allow him to borrow this one, which was an expensive and beautiful weapon. It had taken time and a good deal of eloquence on his part, but eventually his lordship was persuaded to lend it to him. If he returned without it, all hell would break loose. Still kneeling on the damp grass, he pressed his knuckles to his forehead and tried to remember where he had last seen it. Was he carrying it when he was running? somehow, he didn't think so. Had he dropped it whilst he was running? Possibly. There was only one way to find out; he had to retrace his steps back to the guardroom. But which way had he come? He knew of three roads that led from the guardroom to the hangars. He couldn't search them all and anyway, in this darkness, he could pass within a couple of feet of the weapon and not see it. Oh lord, what a mess. He banged his forehead with his clenched fists. 'Think, damn you, think,' he muttered savagely.

He began with his arrival at the guardroom. Yes, he had it then, he remembered laying it across his knees as he squatted on the steps. Once more, he forced himself to see those unearthly shapes gliding silently towards him and his spine tingled again at the memory. Saw himself leap to his feet and heard the double clatter as the shotgun and torch fell from his knees.

'That's it,' he shouted at the stars, 'now I remember.'

But instantly his elation turned to despair. Retrieving the weapon meant returning to the spot from whence he had made such a hasty departure. He shook his head. 'Not on your nelly', he muttered emphatically. He would wait until it was light, then go back. But no, that was no use. What if a farm hand found it before then? It would disappear as quickly as a rabbit bolting down its burrow. For a fleeting moment he saw a picture of himself standing abjectly, his head bowed, receiving the full blast of his lordship's wrath and, with a despairing groan, he stood up and began the long, lonely walk back to the guardroom.

When he was within a few yards of his objective, he stopped and listened. Only the occasional rustle of leaves, agitated by a fitful breeze, disturbed the quiet of the night. The guardroom, a shell of its original structure, stood stark and forbidding and Ralph, breathing deeply in an effort to stem the remnants of courage that were rapidly ebbing away, took a few more hesitant steps, then stopped, looked and listened afresh. Despite the cool of the night, he was perspiring freely. He ran a dry tongue over dry lips and wiped clammy palms on his trousers;

then, taking a deep breath, somewhat deeper than the rest, he set off again, his footsteps scrunching with unnatural loudness on the gravel road.

Now, the guardroom stood before him, black and ominously silent. Through one of the shattered windows he could see the stars peeping through a gaping hole in the roof, and over the verandah, the rotting signboard, upon which could still be discerned the faded lettering, GUARDROOM.

Ralph cast an anxious eye in the direction of the access road, then began his search. Almost immediately he saw it, the starlight glinting faintly on the twin barrels. With a cry of joy, he gathered up the weapon and gave the stock a long, resounding kiss. Oh, what a blessed relief. He cast about for the torch and, eventually, discovered it lodged under the verandah steps.

With the recovery of his torch, Ralph's courage took an upwards turn and he chided himself for being such a bloody fool. Perhaps he had imagined it after all. Everything looked perfectly normal now. Nevertheless, like a pilot who must quickly return to the air after a crash, he had to purge himself, once and for all, of the horrors of this place, otherwise he would never be able to return there at night again. And Ralph didn't like the idea of a no-go area on the estate.

So, crooking the shotgun under his arm, he walked confidently towards the access road, paused at the remnants of the old barrier and swept his torch through a 180 degree arc. Nothing unusual showed up in its beam and, with a grunt of satisfaction, he returned to the guardroom.

Now for the final test. He clutched the shotgun tightly, mounted the verandah steps and paused in the doorway as he shone his torch around the room. A wooden counter faced him and, to his right, his torch revealed two doorways that had long since lost their doors and now gaped darkly open. He skirted the counter and picked his way carefully over the rubble-strewn floor to the door on the right. His torch picked out a small room, empty except for a single cracked and grimy handbasin clinging tenaciously to the wall, and a floor littered with debris. The place reeked of stale excrement. Wrinkling his nose, Ralph turned his attention to the other opening and shone his torch into a small corridor with three doorless rooms opening to the right. He stepped over some bricks and pieces of timber and cautiously peeped into the first room. A small barred window faced him, but his attention was immediately drawn to something that moved in the corner. Pointing his torch, he took a few paces forward and froze.

A man's form floated in a sitting position, a foot or so above the floor and, as he watched, it slowly rose and straightened up. He could see it better now and his heart almost stopped at the sight. It was as if he were looking at an X-ray plate, the bones and arteries clearly visible. Almost sick with horror, Ralph saw that some of the bones were horribly broken and the limbs dripped blood. The thing glided away from him and stopped at the far wall, under the barred window. Then, its mouth opened and a thin piping scream issued forth.

For the second time that night, Ralph uttered a low moan, but this time had the presence of mind to hold on tightly to the torch and shotgun. He turned, stumbled over some bricks, crashed into the counter and fled blindly into the night, fear lending wings to his feet and, ever with him, the sound of that horrible scream and the memory of that ghastly, bloodstained apparition.

Ten minutes later, old Sam, his haversack stuffed to the brim and slapping his side rhythmically, passed through the old barrier and walked jauntily down the access road.

# Chapter 5

A t the sound of George's scream, the flickering aura surrounding the apparition, brightened and the cell was bathed in a blue radiance then, the form melted into the cell door and vanished.

George stood transfixed to the wall, his eyes glued to the spot where the form had dematerialised. It had gone out like a switched-off television set, the small spot in the centre gradually fading away until it disappeared altogether. Slowly, his muscles relaxed, only to tighten again at the first rising note of the 'all clear'. Surprisingly, the prolonged wail of the siren brought with it a sense of comfort, almost normality, and George's fear gave way to blazing anger.

Striding across to the cell door, he grasped the bars and shook them violently. 'Let me out, damn you,' he yelled, 'get me out of this place.'

There was no response and the outer door remained firmly closed. Once again he rattled the door and yelled into the corridor. 'Let me out, let me out,' but with the same result.

Setting his jaw firmly, he strode over to the bed and manoeuvred it on its castors until the foot was against the door; then, muttering savagely, 'Damn you to hell, you will let me out,' he began to bang the bed against the door. The cell shook with the force of the repeated blows and it wasn't long before George's strategy produced the required response. The outer door was flung open and the angry stamp of feet sounded in the corridor. A key rattled in the lock, and George hastily withdrew the bed as the cell door crashed back on its hinges.

'What the hell is all this racket about?'

Sgt. Hawkins stood framed in the doorway, his face flushed

with anger. George stood at the top of the bed and faced the irate sergeant, his slowly dissipating anger leaving him coldly composed.

'By God, Sgt. Hawkins,' he said, evenly, 'I'll see you suffer for this. I've been pounced upon by a band of hooligans in RAF uniforms, dragged here manacled with a Sten in my ribs, forced to suffer the indignity of search and interrogation, then locked up while all you bastards clear off to a shelter. And that's not all . . .' he shuddered at the memory, 'this bloody place is haunted. I've been frightened out of my wits by some . . . something that came through that door. Yes, sergeant, *through* that door,' he emphasised in answer to the sergeant's raised eyebrow. 'And if you think I'm staying here a moment longer, you're crazy.' He started to push past the sergeant and was grabbed by powerful hands, raised off his feet and hurled onto the bed.

'Now listen to me, mister.' Sgt. Hawkins lowered his face to within a few inches of George's. 'I've had just about as much as I can take tonight, and the next peep out of you will be your last.' His voice quavered with controlled anger. 'You'll stay here until I let you out, damn you. Now,' he stood up, 'I'm going to get some kip and I suggest you do the same; you'll need to be wide awake to fool old Jenkins. He's a subtle bastard is that one. They say he's got a heart somewhere, but no one's been able to find it yet. I'll come for you at eight sharp.' As he turned to leave, George said, 'Sgt. Hawkins, do you think I'm an enemy agent?'

The sergeant studied him thoughtfully. 'Dunno, chum, that's not for me to say but,' he gave George a lopsided grin, 'there sure as hell is something strange about you.' And, with that parting shot, he closed the door, locked it and stomped down the corridor. The outer door slammed and George was once more left to his own devices.

'Well,' he muttered to himself, 'that didn't get you very far, did it?' But he felt better. Ghost though the sergeant might be, he was infinitely preferable to that other thing that had invaded his cell and scared the living daylights out of him.

Two types of ghost! George laughed mirthlessly as he pushed

31

the bed back against the wall. Up to now, he hadn't even believed in the existence of one. He flopped onto the bed and stared moodily up at the ceiling.

It had to be a nightmare; things like this just don't happen. Had it been something to do with the accident? Perhaps he hadn't escaped unharmed after all. Maybe a blow on the head was giving him hallucinations. He thought about that; pinched himself, felt the cold frame of the bed and rejected the idea. No, all this was real alright but, on the other hand, how the hell could it be? This was 1978 not 1940. Could he have entered a time warp and been hurled back four decades? Science fiction was full of such tales, but then, that was fiction, wasn't it? There was no evidence that such things existed, but neither was there evidence for the existence of ghosts. But, of the two impossible explanations, George favoured the latter. Those eyes and the absence of reflections in the mirror, not to mention that other . . . thing. George's skin crawled and he switched his thoughts to a more pressing problem.

Those notes. He must have a rational explanation for them before he faced Sqn. Ldr. Jenkins. He closed his eyes and his brow creased in furrows of concentration. After a while, the creases disappeared and he curled up with a satisfied sigh, a small, enigmatic smile tugging at the corners of his lips.

It was eight o'clock on the dot when the keys rattled in the lock and the cell door opened. The obligatory 'Wakey, wakey,' dragged George from a fitful, dream-filled sleep. He blinked resentfully at the bulky form of Sgt. Hawkins, framed in the doorway.

'On your feet, sunshine.' The voice was almost jovial. 'You can freshen up with these.' He threw a towel-wrapped bundle onto the bed. 'Must have you looking your best for the interview. Breakfast is at 8.15 prompt.' He departed, leaving the door ajar.

George sat on the edge of the bed and ran his fingers over his stubbly chin. Funny, he ought to be half doped, considering the small amount of sleep he'd had, but the initial drowsiness had quickly worn off and now he was wide awake.

Flashes of his dreams kept coming back to him. There was a face bending over him, a huge face, blotting out the stars. Then he seemed to be floating feet first, towards a dark, gaping hole. He had no power over his limbs and could only watch with horror as the huge maw drew closer. Suddenly, he was inside and the hole closed leaving him trapped in utter darkness. More flashes. Lights passing by overhead. Another face bending over him, bandaged like a mummy. Hands clutching at him – something placed over his nose and mouth. Panic, then darkness again. George tried to remember more, but already, the dream was fading and in a few moments, it was but a vague memory, lingering only as a perfume lingers in a room in the wake of the wearer. He pondered on the significance of his dreams, then stretched luxuriously, picked up the bundle and walked out of the cell into the guardroom.

The place hummed with activity. Corporal Phillips was at the counter, busily handing over keys to collectors and obtaining their signature. Leading Aircraftsman (L.A.C.) Billings was making up a bed in the corner, while another airman – a stranger, whom George took to be the one that had challenged them at the gate – was applying the final polish to his boots. Of Sgt. Hawkins there was no sign. George called out a general 'Good morning,' but apart from turning and staring at him with those strange eyes, the men made no response. He shrugged and entered the ablutions.

The room contained one handbasin with a small shelf and chipped mirror above and two lavatories with doors that left a gap of a foot or so above the floor. He looked at the doors thoughtfully and decided that he had no need to avail himself of their facilities. Mildly surprised, he turned and gazed at his reflection in the mirror while the basin filled with water. For one who had been through so much in the last six hours, the face that stared back at him looked remarkably fresh and alert. Only small vestiges remained of the deep lines that had previously etched his forehead and the sides of his mouth, and dark hair was beginning to replace the grey at his temples. He poked his tongue out. This was a morning ritual which was usually followed by a grimace and an immediate retraction, but today it remained extended while he savoured its unusual pinkness. Something was happening to him; his body was undergoing a metamorphosis but, far from being pleased at the result, his youthful appearance only served to increase his apprehension.

Water began to overflow the basin and slop onto the floor. He hastily turned off the taps and reduced the amount of water to the required level; then, pushing his fears into the background, he began to soap his hands. Sgt. Hawkins had supplied most of the requisites except a toothbrush but, after shaving awkwardly with a cut-throat razor, he squeezed some toothpaste onto his finger and rubbed it over his teeth. His toilet finished, he wrapped the requisites neatly in the towel and stepped once more into the guardroom.

The night guard had departed and the service police (SPs) had taken over. There were three of them: a sergeant, a corporal and an L.A.C., all looking smart in their white-capped hats, white blancoed webbing belts and shoulder straps, knife edged creases in trousers tucked into white gaiters and boots with gleaming toe caps. A white lanyard tucked under the sergeant's shoulder strap, terminated at the butt of a .38 Smith and Wesson revolver which poked out of the buttoned-up flap of a hip holster.

'Ah, good morning, Mr Reynolds.' The sergeant turned as George approached and the now familiar white eyes rested on him. He was smiling.

'I trust you slept well.' The accent was Scottish.

George nodded, his eyes on his wallet lying open on the counter. The sergeant picked it up and handed it to George.

'I believe this is yours, sir.'

He seemed a pleasant enough chap and the respectful 'sir' had not gone unnoticed, but George remained on his guard. Sometimes these 'pleasant' bastards could be the worst.

'Thank you, sergeant.' George placed the bundle on the bench, took the wallet and thumbed through the contents.

'Are these what you are looking for?'

The sergeant produced an envelope from a drawer. Inside was his money, RAFVR identity card and driving licence.

34

'I'm afraid we'll have to retain these until the matter of your identity is cleared up.'

George nodded. 'Where is Sergeant Hawkins?'

'Raising the flag. He'll be back soon.'

As if in response to the sergeant's cue, there came the sharp blast of a whistle, to be followed moments later by two more in quick succession. George glanced at the clock on the wall.

'Eight fifteen. He's late; should have been up at eight.'

The sergeant shot him a sharp glance, then grinned. 'Not his fault, sir, the orderly officer was late. There's been a bit of a flap on down at the dispersal this morning.' Without offering any further explanation, he continued in the manner of a well-trained butler. 'Now, sir, if you will return to your cell, your breakfast awaits you on the bed.' Grinning at the sergeant's elaborate courtesy, George allowed himself to be escorted back to the cell. Just before he left, the sergeant paused at the door and subjected George to a hard scrutiny.

'Sgt. Hawkins thinks you're a Nazi,' he said, eventually 'me? I'm not so sure, but those notes will take a lot of explaining.'

George sighed. 'Those notes, sergeant, are the least of my worries.'

The service police sergeant seemed about to pursue the subject, but changed his mind and merely said, 'Eat your breakfast, it's getting cold.'

George sat on the bed, took the tin lid off the plate and gazed distastefully at the contents. One slice of streaky bacon, a rubbery egg, fried to extinction, a few baked beans and a triangle of fried bread, all reposing in a film of rapidly hardening fat. He pushed the plate away in disgust. The tea was typical cookhouse brew – weak, tepid and not enough sugar for his liking. After a few sips, he decided he'd had enough of that, too. What the hell, he thought gloomily, I'm not hungry. He placed the tray on the floor, stretched out on the bed, and stared moodily at the ceiling.

Then, without any warning, the pain came. Wave after wave of excruciating agony wracked his body. His muscles, responding to an involuntary spasm, flexed to contract his limbs, but some force held them securely pinned. Faces appeared on the ceiling, anxious faces, moving, interchanging, fading away and returning again. Sounds filled his head: a rhythmic pumping, the occasional clash of metal on metal, a high-pitched bleeping and voices – vague unintelligible mutterings which seemed to convey a sense of urgency.

Now the pain was subsiding and in its place came a feeling of lassitude and well-being. The sounds grew muted; he felt himself floating, drifting away into a dense, swirling, blood-red mist. A persistent, nagging voice kept telling him to fight. He tried desperately to respond and the mists cleared a little, only to be replaced by the pain, crushing, unbearable. Better to relax, he was too tired to fight. Once again, the mists closed in, clinging, enveloping. He was drawn into their murky depths, faster and faster, deeper and deeper, blood red turning to purple, purple to indigo and, in the moment before total blackness overwhelmed him, the fading sound of the high-pitched bleep turned to a steady, unwavering note.

George sat up suddenly, the scream bubbling in his throat changing to a long-drawn-out groan as he recognised his surroundings. He clasped his head in his hands and thought, 'I must be going mad.' It was that dream again; no sane person had dreams like that. They were the images conjured up by a demented mind. But of what had he dreamed? He was aware that it had been something frightful but, like the first, it had now faded away, leaving behind only the residual fear and horror.

He slipped off the bed and paced the room with quick, agitated steps. Why was he here? The whole thing was crazy. Could it have been a result of the accident? Was this his ghost pacing the floor? Was he one of them out there? How otherwise did they seem so real and substantial? No, he shook his head savagely; that way really did lead to madness. There had to be some other explanation. He sat on the bed and lowered his face onto his hands.

'Oh God,' he muttered distraughtly, 'please let there be another answer.' But the thought persisted and he was forced to admit that it would explain a lot.

36

'Right, Mr Reynolds.' Sgt. Hawkins' voice dragged him back from his gloomy thoughts. 'Shall we go? The sooner I deliver you to Jenkins, the sooner I can get some real kip.'

George looked up with relief. He desperately needed something to occupy his mind and he was eagerly looking forward to the forthcoming interview. So, it was with rising spirits that he followed the sergeant out of the guardroom and paused on the verandah, blinking in the bright sunlight. The sight that confronted him brought with it a throat-constricting wave of nostalgia.

Once more, he was an eighteen-year-old sprog (raw recruit), posted to his first operational unit. Everything was as he remembered it. The wide roads and neatly trimmed grass verges, bordered with avenues of cherry blossom and laburnum; the solid, squat administration buildings; the 'H' type barrack blocks, surrounding the parade ground, over which the distinctive RAF ensign hung limp in the still morning air. To his left, and separated by the sports field, stood two buildings, one slightly more imposing than the other, which George recognised by their flower-decked frontages and nearby tennis courts, as the officers' and sergeants' messes, while, towards the airfield and towering over the intermediate buildings, stood the massive silhouettes of four aircraft hangars.

The wide road, separating the guardroom from station headquarters (SHQ), bustled with traffic, both entering and leaving the station. Right now there was a bit of a snarl-up caused by a low loader, ferrying a complete wing section, trying to negotiate an island, aided by a couple of airmen shouting instructions and obscenities at the unfortunate driver while, behind him, the driver of a three-ton lorry added his strident voice to the confusion.

An old banger roared into the station, crammed full of aircrew, some still clutching bottles and various items of feminine apparel. They cheered and whistled loudly as the driver, neatly avoiding the congestion, circumnavigated the island the wrong way around, causing a motor cyclist to swerve wildly, mount the curb and finish up sitting in the middle of a flower bed. He shook his fist at the retreating banger and Sgt. Hawkins showed his disapproval with a loud sniff. He grabbed George's arm.

'Come on,' he said brusquely, taking advantage of a break in the traffic, and propelling George across the road.

'You don't have to hold my arm,' said George, crossly. 'I won't try to escape.' Sgt. Hawkins merely tightened his grip and increased his pace.

Ignoring the main entrance, traditionally reserved for officers, he led George to a small door at the side of the building. A narrow passageway led them to a long office-lined corridor with a broad staircase facing the main doors. Sgt. Hawkins took him to a door with a sign, extending into the hall, marked S.Ad.O. On the door, the name Sqn. Ldr R. L. Jenkins, DSO, DFC, was emblazoned in gold lettering.

Sgt. Hawkins rapped on the door and a voice answered, 'Come.' He opened the door, ushered George into the room, closed the door quietly then snapped to attention and saluted.

The officer, seated at a sturdy oak desk, was laying down the law on the telephone in a noticeably Welsh accent.

'I don't care what they've been through, David. This is a military unit and I will not have them behaving like hooligans. They are officers and I expect them to set an example to the men. Now, they're your men, so I'll leave you to deal with them this time, but, I warn you, David, any more of this disgraceful behaviour and I'll not only throw the book at the offenders, but your head will be on the chopping block, too.'

The earpiece squawked indignantly, and Sqn. Ldr. Jenkins snapped impatiently, 'That's your problem, David.' He looked at George, 'I have one of my own right here now. Look David,' his voice dropped to a more conciliatory tone, 'I don't expect them to behave like ladies at a vicar's tea party but, in future, if they want to let off steam, for God's sake tell them not to do it in front of SHQ.' The earpiece squawed again – apologetically.

'Right, right you do that.' He slammed the phone down, stared at it moodily for a moment, then transferred his gaze to George.

The first thing one noticed about Sqn. Ldr. Jenkins was a vivid red scar that ran from the left temple to the cheekbone, tugging at the eye and pulling it in a downward direction, the next, his hair, luxuriant, wavey and snow white. Seated, it was difficult to assess his height, but he was heavily built, with a physique that reminded George of an athlete who had gone to seed. He was probably in his late thirties, early forties. Some other facet of his appearance bugged George but, for the life of him, he couldn't think what it was, and it wasn't until he met the officer's steady gaze that he realised what it was. The eyes that were studying him so closely were a steely blue.

No blind, expressionless whiteness there, just honest-to-goodness, normal eyes. On an impulse, he turned to look at Sgt. Hawkins. One quick glance was enough to tell him that they were now a warm brown.

Before he had time to assess the implications of this transformation, the officer, still staring at George, addressed the sergeant.

'So, Sergeant Hawkins, you have caught yourself an enemy agent.' This statement of fact, spoken slowly and softly, conveyed a menacing undertone and the sergeant permitted himself a rapid glance at the officer before resuming his fixed gaze ahead.

'I believe so, sir.'

'You believe so, sergeant?' He looked at Sgt. Hawkins in amazement. 'Do you mean to tell me that you are not sure?' His tone of voice was mildly reproachful, as if someone he had trusted implicitly had let him down.

Sgt. Hawkins, recognising the warning symptoms, stole another hasty glance at the officer and licked his lips nervously.

'The search party found this man hiding in a ditch at the side of the approach road, and the fact that he was skulking there at 2.30 in the morning, gave me sufficient reason to detain him. The brief interrogation I was able to conduct before the sirens went, confirmed that he had something to hide; he evaded most of my direct questions and seemed to be in a confused condition. I got the impression that he wasn't sure where he was or why he was here.'

Sqn. Ldr. Jenkins nodded understandingly. 'All of which, of

course, left you in no doubt that he was a Nazi spy.' It was painfully obvious that the officer was sadistically playing with the sergeant as a cat plays with a mouse and, although he must have inwardly seethed, Sgt. Hawkins' voice betrayed no emotion when he answered.

'It is not within my jurisdiction to pass judgement in cases like that, sir. That, if I may say so, is your province. I might also remind you, with respect, that a tradesman is not a trained interrogater, but, in my opinion, for what it's worth, this man warrants the attention of a special investigator.' He unbuttoned his top pocket and pulled out the envelope containing George's money and ID card.

'These articles were found on the prisoner during the search. I leave you to draw your own conclusion as to their significance.' He placed the envelope on the desk, then stepped back and resumed his rigid stance.

Sqn. Ldr. Jenkins looked at the envelope, then back at the sergeant, a small smile tugging at the corner of his lips.

'Well now, sergeant, that was quite a speech. Well done.' No sarcasm there now, he seemed genuinely pleased. 'I congratulate you on your conduct during this interview, it was exemplary, I only wish there were more like you. You wouldn't believe the inarticulate idiots I sometimes have to contend with. Now, sergeant, you must be tired so I won't detain you any longer.'

Sgt. Hawkins glanced at George. 'But, sir . . .'

The smile remained but the eyes grew hard. 'That will be all, thank you, sergeant.'

Sgt. Hawkins saluted impeccably, did a smart about turn and marched out of the room, sensibly retiring whilst he was still ahead.

'Sit down, Mr Reynolds,' the Station Adjutant Officer waved a hand at a nearby chair. George pulled it a little nearer the desk and sank into it gratefully, regarding the officer warily.

He pushed a silver casket towards George.

'Cigarette?'

'Er, thank you.'

George raised the lid, selected a cigarette and noted the

brand, Gold Flake. He lit it with the officer's proffered lighter and drew down a lungful of smoke, savouring the flavour. He relaxed, crossed his legs and awaited the officer's next move.

Sqn. Ldr. Jenkins was looking at him curiously. 'You know, Mr Reynolds, I have been misinformed. I was led to believe that you were an older man. "In his fifties" I think Sgt. Hawkins said, but, to me, you don't look much past forty.'

'The process does have that effect,' said George.

Sqn. Ldr Jenkins pricked up his ears. 'Process?' he said, frowning, 'what process?'

George pointed at the envelope. 'I think you'd better look in there,' he said enigmatically.

Still frowning, the officer extended his arm to pick up the envelope, then changed his mind and pressed a switch on the intercom.

'A girl's voice answered. 'Yes, sir.'

'Come in here, will you, Cpl. Miller and bring your notebook and pencil. I want you to take a few notes.'

'Yes, sir.'

He flicked the switch and sighed. 'I'm beginning to think that Sgt. Hawkins was right; there *is* more to you than meets the eye. Oh, I don't mean you're a spy or any of that rot. No self-respecting agent would have had his pockets crammed full of articles calculated to arouse suspicion; but there is something strange about you, George Reynolds, and before we're through here, I'll know what it is. You're an enigma and I don't like mysteries. I like everything to be cut and dried.' He smiled sadly. 'You're not going to give me a hard time are you, Mr Reynolds?'

'On the contrary, squadron leader.' George shook his head gravely. 'I shall be an open book, although, whether I can convince you that I am telling the truth is another matter.'

Sqn. Ldr. Jenkins grunted noncommittally. 'I can see it's going to be one of those days. Come,' he called out, in answer to a soft knock.

If George had cherished any thoughts that his quota of shocks had been exhausted, the sight of the girl entering the room dispelled any such illusions. About 5 ft 2 in, slim, round-faced with large brown eyes, her long dark hair wrapped around a ribbon, WAAF style, George recognised her immediately. Her name was Judy Miller and her face fitted exactly the image he had retained in his memory, still clear and well defined, despite the passage of years. They had met at a dance at the Hammersmith Palais one evening in 1942. To their mutual surprise, they had discovered that they were both stationed at RAF Manston, in Kent but, until that wartime evening their paths had never crossed. They had gone out together a lot after that, and their relationship had developed into something more than friendship.

George's throat constricted and he turned his head to hide the tears that sprang to his eyes, as he remembered the day when, running with him to catch the last bus back to camp, she had run into the road directly in the path of a passing lorry. He could still hear the sickening thud as the hard metal bonnet hit her soft, yielding body, the screech of the tyres as the lorry mounted the pavement and the shattering of glass as it ploughed through a shop window. Before the ambulance arrived, she had died, cradled in his arms.

This then was his proof; no doubt remained in his mind now. This was indeed a ghost station, staffed with people long since dead. The only question remaining unanswered now was – was he one of them?

# Chapter 6

'Order, order.' Lord Redford banged his gavel on the table until the uproar in the village hall had subsided, leaving only a couple of pockets of muted discontent. He glared down from the stage at the score or so people occupying the two front rows of seats and banged the gavel again until he had their full attention.

'Thank you.' He smoothed his handlebar moustache, stuck his thumbs into his waistcoat pockets and continued to glare at them for a few more moments.

He was a stout man, middle aged with a florid complexion and slightly bulging eyes, topped by bushy eyebrows. He was flanked at the table by two men. One, smartly dressed with a military bearing, was in his late fifties but still retained much of his youthful good looks. The other, seated on his left, was somewhat older, tall and gaunt, wearing clerical garb and a mournful expression. Right now, Lord Redford's moustache bristled and two angry red spots suffused his chubby cheeks.

'I repeat, all this talk about ghosts is a lot of superstitious nonsense. I have agreed to chair this meeting only because Clive here,' – he nodded at the gentleman on his right – 'can be very persuasive and I was intrigued to hear what he had to say; but, damn it all, there's a natural explanation for everything, and I'm sure if we probe deep enough, one can be found for these so-called manifestations.'

'Are you saying, then, my lord, that the thing that I saw in the old guardroom existed only in my imagination?' Ralph Morgan stared at his lordship sullenly.

'Aye, and how do you explain those see-through figures that keep flitting in and out of my pub, scaring the pants – beggin'

43

your pardon, ladies – off the missus and kids, not to mention me customers. You've all seen them, haven't you?' Albert Brewster, landlord of *The Redford Arms*, and an aptly named publican, stood up and turned to his regulars for support. A chorus of 'ayes' greeted his last remark and old Jack Hicks, his lordship's head gardener, enlarged upon the point.

'I were settin' in the snug wi' old Jim here, one night last May it were, suppin' my pint all peaceful like, when a couple of the cheeky bu . . .' he corrected himself at a glare from his wife, 'beggers came and plonked themselves right down beside us. I tell you, if old Jim hadn't seen them, too, I'd have signed the pledge there and then.' He nodded in emphatic agreement with himself.

Alice Tibble, matronly proprietress of the village sub-post office and general store – and also, one-time nanny to the Redford family – stood up, folded her arms and stared grimly at his lordship over her pince-nez spectacles.

'Are you also saying, then, Peter Redford that I, too, am subject to hallucinations?' Lord Redford blanched and his moustache wilted visibly.

'Of course not, Alice my dear, it's just that . . .'

'It's just that you're a pompous old fathead, Peter Redford. You believed in ghosts well enough when you were little; claimed you saw one in the West Wing; La, la,' she fluttered her hands in the air, 'what a fuss you made then, wouldn't sleep without a night-light for ages after that. Then there was the time . . .'

'Alice, please.' His lordship 'humphed' and wriggled with embarrassment. 'After all, I *was* only a child.'

Alice sniffed. 'Some children are more perceptive than many adults I can name. The fact remains, Peter, that Wing Commander Prescott was concerned enough to call this meeting and to ask you to chair it. These good people are concerned, too, and so am I, and I think the least you can do is to give them a fair hearing.'

Lord Redford smiled at Alice affectionately. 'You're an old blackmailer, Nanny.'

Alice's eyes softened momentarily at the mention of that

well-loved title. It had been a long time since anyone had called her that; then she stiffened and drew herself upright.

'And you won't get around me that way either, Peter Redford.'

Lord Redford shook his head and sighed. 'All right, Alice, you win. Now sit down, my dear, and I'll try to keep an open mind.' Alice nodded a magnanimous acceptance of his capitulation and sat down, primly smoothing her skirts.

'Well then.' Lord Redford flicked an imaginary speck of dust from his sleeve. 'Who else has seen these . . . these apparitions?'

A chair scraped in the middle of the second row and a long-haired, sallow-faced youth dressed in scruffy jeans and a none-too-clean T-shirt shuffled to his feet.

'I have me lud.' He deliberately gave it the judicial pronunciation, slavishly aping his generation's contempt for authority.

Lord Redford gazed upon him distastefully. 'This is not a court of law, young fella, and I am not a judge.'

The youth stuck his hands in his jeans and smirked insolently. 'You could have fooled me the way you were banging away at that table just now.'

His lordship's moustache entered the first stages of an uncontrollable bristle and the two ominous pink spots returned to his cheeks. He glanced at Alice and controlled himself with an effort.

'Might I say something, my lord?' Sergeant Price, the local representative of the law stood up. 'I asked this young lad to attend this meeting so that he could repeat to you the story he told me last night – or early this morning, I should say.' Peter Redford nodded and the sergeant resumed his seat.

'With your lordship's permission, there is one thing I'd like to clear up before we continue.' Bob Alwood, the garage proprietor, grabbed a handful of the lad's ample locks and a ham-like fist was shoved under his nose.

'Now, me lad, I'd take it kindly if you were to show more respect to his lordship because, if you don't, I'll punch your teeth down your throat, one by one.' He twisted the hair a little tighter and the youth squealed with pain.

45

'Now, apologise to his lordship – go on,' he gave the hair another tug. The youth squealed again. 'You're hurting me.' The grip tightened on his hair. 'I'll hurt you a damned sight more if you don't do as you're told.'

'OK, OK, I'm sorry.'

'Say it to his lordship.'

'I'm sorry, your lordship.'

Bob reluctantly released his grip of the youth's hair. 'Now, carry on and mind your manners,' he growled.

A ripple of approval came from the assembled villagers and the youth, resentful but subdued, tenderly rubbed the back of his head.

His lordship, making a poor attempt to hide his satisfaction, addressed the crestfallen lad.

'And now, young fella, perhaps you will begin by telling us your name.'

'Andrew Stockton, my lord.' The last two words almost choked him.

His lordship pricked up his ears. 'Any relation to Trevor Stockton, the estate agent?'

The youth nodded sullenly. 'He's my father – er, my lord.'

'Hmmm,' His lordship gazed at the lad, taking in his unkempt appearance and shaggy locks and wondered sadly – not for the first time – what kind of society it was that produced dropouts like Andrew. He would never understand how, instead of making the most of the God-given gift of youth, todays' kids had to squander it all on making themselves look as ugly and disreputable as possible – and with no apparent thought for the feelings of their parents. He knew Mabel and Trevor Stockton; had met them on occasions at the golf club, and knew them to be sincere and decent people, still very much in love with each other. Andrew must be a great disappointment to them. Ah, well, he shrugged inwardly, it wasn't his problem. Thank God Tony had turned out alright. He 'humphed' to clear his mind of such thoughts, and resumed his questioning.

'And now, Andrew, you say you have also seen these – er, apparitions?'

46

Andrew nodded, more composed now and a little of his cockiness returning. Bob Alwood kept a watchful eye on him.

'Yeah, just after me and this bird found that wrecked Mini and that bloody body . . .' A growl from behind prompted Andrew to hastily qualify that statement. 'Er, by that I mean he was covered in blood, my lord.'

Lord Redford would dearly have liked to ask him what he was doing in such a remote spot in the small hours of the morning, but knowing the capacity of today's youth to shock, he was reluctant to press the subject.

'I don't know how long he had been there,' Andrew continued, 'but the old boy was in a bad way; Christ, there was blood everywhere. I felt his pulse but there was no sign of a heartbeat. I thought he was a goner. Sandra was leaning against a tree; she'd just been sick and I could see she was about to throw a fit or something, so I grabbed her and we legged it through the woods, taking the short cut down Archer's Way. Then I saw these strange, wispy shapes, away to the right, flitting among the trees and glowing with a cold, blue light . . .'

Ralph Morgan sprang to his feet. 'There, what did I tell you, my lord?' He interjected triumphantly, 'apart from that other horror, that's exactly as I described them.'

Lord Redford was forced to agree. 'It was, Ralph, uncannily like it.' A tiny doubt was beginning to gnaw away at his dogmatic disbelief. That the description of these sightings, given by two people without prior contact with each other, should agree so accurately was surely beyond coincidence. He mentally chalked one up to the opposition and told Andrew to continue.

Andrew shot Ralph a grateful glance. He hadn't wanted to come to this meeting in the first place; was convinced that no one would believe his story. He had been cheered by what Albert Brewster and one or two others had said, but now he had a strong ally, one who had seen almost exactly what he had seen – and in the same vicinity – and was prepared to back him up. Perhaps because of this thought, he no longer felt it necessary to be constantly on the defensive. When he next spoke, it was in a cultured voice with no trace of the slang and jargon that had previously spattered his sentences.

'I stopped and called out to Sandra to come back, but she was running down the path as if all the shades in hell were after her.' He gave a twisted grin. 'And for all I know, perhaps they were, too. I guess if I'd had any sense, I'd have been a half a mile ahead of her but curiosity got the better of me and I hid behind a mass of brambles and waited to see what would happen next.'

In spite of himself, Lord Redford was beginning to feel a grudging admiration for the lad. He grunted his approval.

'That was very brave of you, Andrew.'

Andrew snorted. 'Brave nothing. I was scared stiff and shaking like a leaf. Anyhow, as I watched, the wispy shapes began to drift together and form a group which seemed to expand and contract, swaying all the time like . . . like sea-plants caught up in the movement of the waters. Then I heard sounds, strange whisperings and ululations, sometimes hardly audible, sometimes rising to a twittering crescendo.'

'Then they began to disperse and I noticed that one of them was heading my way. I don't mind telling you, the only reason I didn't take to my heels there and then was because I was petrified. It made no sound as it approached, no crunching of leaves, no snapping of twigs, only a silent, eerie glide.'

He paused for effect and looked at the faces of the villagers. Alice, who had punctuated the narrative here and there with a shocked 'How dreadful,' and an occasional, 'My, my,' was looking very pale. Ralph was nodding knowledgeably as one who had shared a similar experience, while old Sam Bassett, arms folded and feet resting on the chair in front, smiled quietly to himself, content with the knowledge that, if he wished, he too could tell a tale or two. The remainder, eyes fixed on Andrew, listened with rapt attention. Satisfied that his pause had the desired effect, Andrew continued.

'Another thing, too. Some of the trees in its path, it just passed clean through, others it bypassed normally and then, there were occasions when it deviated from its course for no apparent reason, almost as if it were skirting obstacles that were no longer there.'

'As it drew nearer, I felt a distinct drop in the temperature –

just as the air cools rapidly when a cloud passes in front of the sun – and the atmosphere became heavily charged. I felt my hair creep and my skin tingled as if it were being punctured by a thousand needles. I brought my fingers together experimentally and tiny blue flashes leapt between them. I'm convinced that if anyone were foolish enough to touch one of those things, they would be electrocuted. It passed within ten feet or so of me and, although my view was limited, there was an instant when I got a good look at it.' He paused once more and awaited the expected reaction, but this time they were in no mood for interruptions and there were soon calls of 'Get on with it, then,' while Lord Redford said impatiently, 'Speak up, lad, we haven't got all day.'

Andrew bowed gravely and Bob Alwood eyed him suspiciously. 'You must understand, my lord, that the form was never really stable. It flickered constantly and the blue aura surrounding it occasionally expanded and glowed to such an extent that the figure vanished in the brightness. But there came a moment, when the glow was at its lowest ebb and the flickering not quite so noticeable, that the figure momentarily stabilised and I could just make out its shape. It was a serviceman. He was dressed in wartime gear, complete with tin hat and all the other gubbins that they wore during the early days of the war. He held a rifle, pointing forward, and walked in a crouching attitude treading the ground cautiously. And that's all I saw,' Andrew shrugged, 'for at that moment, something fat and furry crawled over my legs. I instinctively leapt to my feet and rolled into a small gully, finishing up in a bed of nettles.' He grinned ruefully, 'I guess it just wasn't my night. By the time I'd climbed out of the gully, there was no sign of matey or any of the others for that matter so, what with one thing and another, I decided that the time was ripe to make myself scarce. When I reached the village, I banged on the door and awoke Sergeant Price, told him about the accident and, after he'd phoned the hospital, I told him a little of what I'd seen. I was supping a cup of tea when the ambulance arrived, so I piled aboard and directed them to the scene of the accident. The poor chap was in a hell of a mess, but he was still alive, although the ambulance men didn't seem to give much for his chances. And that's it. Can I go now, my lord?'

Lord Redford shook his head. 'I'd prefer it if you stayed a little longer, Andrew, I might have to call upon you later in the proceedings.'

Andrew pulled a face and sat down. Little pockets of conversation started up and Albert Brewster's voice rose above the rest.

'My lord, may I speak?'

Once again, Lord Redford's gavel came into action and the chatter subsided. 'You have the floor, Mr Brewster.'

'I can't see that this throws any new light on the subject. We all know that these things are the ghosts of servicemen.' He gave a bitter laugh. 'I've rubbed shoulders with them often enough at the pub not to doubt that. But how are we going to get rid of them? That's what we should be concentrating on.'

'Just a minute, Mr Brewster.' Lord Redford frowned. 'Do you mean that literally or metaphorically – about rubbing shoulders with them, I mean?'

Albert laughed and his ample belly moved up and down rhythmically. 'I mean it literally, my lord; why, I even walked straight through one once before I realised it was there.'

'Then this is surely at variance with the statement that Andrew has just made.' Lord Redford studied his notes. 'Ah yes, here it is. He said, and I quote, "I'm convinced that if anyone were foolish enough to touch one of those things, they would be electrocuted." He put down the notes and looked at Albert. 'Does that sound like the sort of ghost that you are familiar with, Mr Brewster?'

'Well . . . er . . . no,' said Albert, momentarily confused, then incredulously, 'are you telling us, then, that we are dealing with two types of ghost?'

Lord Redford signed. 'A half an hour ago, Mr Brewster, I would have wagered the family fortune on there being no kinds of ghost at all. Now – well, I'm not so sure, not so sure at all.' He shook his head dubiously.

The military looking gentleman on Lord Redford's right

coughed discreetly. 'Perhaps, my lord, at this stage, I should explain to these good people why I have called this meeting.'

Lord Redford gave him a grateful look. 'I was wondering when you were going to come to my rescue, Clive.' He smiled and addressed the villagers.

'Ladies and gentlemen, Wing Commander Prescott will now give you his reasons for calling this meeting. You all know him, so there's no need for further introductions. They're all your's Clive.' He stuck his thumbs in his waistcoat pockets, puffed out his cheeks and settled back thankfully in his chair.

Wing Commander Prescott was a relatively recent addition to the community. He had appeared at the Lewes office of Stockton and Burnett, estate agents, one day five years ago and bought 10 acres of land comprising the old railway halt, water tank, signal box and two fields flanking the old railway approach road. In a short time, he had converted the dilapidated station buildings on the down side into an attractive bungalow, while those on the up side became the garden shop and offices of a flourishing nursery and market garden business, employing five villagers full time.

Nothing was known about him prior to his arrival in the village. He had settled there on retiring from the RAF and, from the start, had joined whole-heartedly in the life of the little community, helping to raise money for the church by organising fetes and supervising outings for the elderly. The young, too, were not forgotten and, once a month this selfsame hall rocked to a local pop group or disco.

On Tuesday and Friday evenings and Sunday mornings, he could be found enjoying a pint of bitter and a chat with some of the regulars in the saloon bar of the 'Redford Arms'. His favourite topic of conversation was the *phantom squadron* as the locals termed the plague of ghostly figures that infested the village and old airfield, and would listen avidly to tales of encounters and visitations.

On many a fine summer day he could be found, a lonely figure, strolling among the derelict buildings of the old airfield and stopping for an occasional chat with the farm hands. 'Enjoying a bout of nostalgia, I wouldn't wonder,' as old Sam

51

put it in one of his more philosophical moments. A well-liked man, then, and accepted with surprising rapidity by the normally insular community but, still something of an enigma.

Now, as he gazed down from the stage at the little group of upturned faces, he wondered how they were going to react to what he was about to tell them. He didn't relish the thought of making a fool of himself, and there was an even chance that he might do so, especially considering the strange phenomena that became apparent to him each time he recounted the events of that day; but this was why he had settled in the village. For five years he had waited for this moment and now, as he had anticipated, things were coming to a head. If these restless spirits were to be freed from their earthly bondage, it was now, and only now, that it could be done. He hitched his chair a little closer to the table and cleared his throat.

'My friends, when I came to live among you, many of you, perhaps, wondered why I chose to settle here of all places. Well, the answer is – to prepare for this very moment.' His audience rustled expectantly and Lord Redford cocked an enquiring eyebrow at him.

'You see, I'm not such a stranger to this village as I have led you to believe. Thirty-eight years ago, in June 1940 to be exact, I was posted to RAF Lynton Down as a fresh young flying officer. I was there on the morning of September 15th when a sneak raid almost totally destroyed the station, killing 90 per cent of its personnel.' Some of the older members of the audience nodded their heads sadly at the wing commander's words, remembering the stray bomb that fell on the village, demolishing the old Redford Arms and six adjacent cottages. Six villagers had died, buried beneath the rubble.

'Something else happened that day – something which I believe to be responsible for these ghosts which have plagued the old airfield and the village for the past thirty-eight years.' Feet scraped the floor as the villagers leaned forward, their interest now thoroughly aroused.

Clive poured some water into a glass and took a couple of quick sips. He shot a quick look towards the entrance doors at the rear of the hall and glanced at his watch before continuing.

'There was a bit of a flap on at the dispersal that morning. Two squadrons had been ordered off to reinforce Biggin Hill and Hornchurch; this left us with just one squadron to cover the whole sector. Skipper was blazing mad; extra load would mean having to fly more sorties and the pilots were very near breaking point, not to mention the groundcrew, who were also in an ugly mood. Morale had sunk to rock bottom of late, mostly because of overwork, bad living conditions, bad food and the intransigence of the station commander who, being a strict disciplinarian, insisted on the station being run on a peacetime basis, with daily parades, 'bull' nights for endless domestic duties and kit inspections. Now, on top of this, after being up half the night combing the countryside for a suspected parachutist, to be dragged out of bed after only a few hours sleep, in order to see the station being denuded of two vital squadrons, was the last straw. Actually, we did bag ourselves a parachutist later that morning. He'd bailed out of that HE one eleven which came down in Burgess Wood. Caught him in the act of trying to pinch a Spit.' He smiled at the memory. 'Cheeky blighter – anyway, there was a hell of a row and Group Captain Bailey, fearing a mutiny, ordered all those not on essential duty to assemble at the station cinema at 10 a.m. for a pep talk, no doubt, and maybe read us the riot act. It was an act of folly which cost the lives of many people. He should have know better than to assemble so many people in one place, especially on a front-line station during wartime. But I digress. It was just after 10 o'clock when the station admin. officer, Squadron Leader Jenkins, walked into the crew room. Following hard on his heels was a sight which almost caused me to cry out aloud in astonishment. He was accompanied by a man, dressed in ill-fitting civvies, whom I judged to be in his late twenties – early thirties, but the astounding thing about it was that, although everything about him was clear-cut and distinct, I could see right through him.'

He paused to take a sip of water and the audience stirred, a buzz of conversation dying away almost as soon as it was born. His lordship leant towards him and whispered, 'Do you mean to tell me, Clive, that there were ghosts in the old airfield even then?'

Clive smiled a little bleakly. 'Well, not exactly, my lord, although I believe it does have a direct bearing on all that has happened since.' He glanced once more at his watch.

'What time do you make it, my lord?'

His lordship pulled out a pocket watch and flicked back the face cover. 'Nine thirty-six.' He snapped the cover back and replaced the watch.

'Are you expecting someone, Clive?'

Clive nodded. 'I am, my lord. She's late and time is of the essence.' His voice carried an agitated edge.

His lordship raised his eyebrows. 'She?'

Clive nodded again but offered no further explanation and his lordship tactfully didn't press the subject.

The Revd. Ian Sinclair's normally lugubrious countenance looked even more mournful than usual. The fact of the matter was, he was bored. For the life of him, he couldn't see why he'd been asked to attend the meeting. Didn't seem to concern him in the slightest and there were so many more important things he could be doing. There was the evening's sermon – that needed polishing up – then there was the hedge to trim and the elderberry wine he was going to make. He dug his hands deeply into his trouser pocket, stretched out his legs and stared moodily at the audience.

Clive Prescott was just about to resume his narrative, when the entrance doors swung open, admitting a woman in her mid-thirties, clad in tweeds, brisk and businesslike of manner, whose comely features were rather spoiled by a severe hairstyle which pulled her dark hair back from a central parting into two buns at the nape of her neck. A pair of those large, fashionable spectacles, ridiculously perched on a small, well-shaped nose, gave her an owl-like appearance. The villagers turned as one to stare at her as she waved at Clive and twenty pairs of eyes followed as she walked down the aisle and mounted the steps leading to the stage.

The three men rose to greet her and Clive, smiling his relief, clasped both her outstretched hands and introduced her to all present as Dorothy Beresford of the Institute of Psychic Research. She smiled a warm, pleasant smile which softened her features and went a long way towards counteracting the self-inflicted severity of her appearance.

'I'm sorry I'm late Clive,' her voice was low, her words only meant for his ears, 'I called in at the hospital to see if there was any further news of Mr Reynolds. It seems he's still in a deep coma. His heart stopped during the operation, but they managed to get it going again. At the moment, he's in intensive care.'

Clive smiled and pressed her hands. A chair was brought for her and she joined the three men at the table. Looking relaxed and happier now that Dorothy Beresford had finally arrived, Clive Prescott once more turned his attention to the villagers.

'Forgive the interruption, ladies and gentlemen; I shall explain Miss Beresford's presence in due course. In the meantime, with your permission, I shall conclude my story. If my behaviour seems a little strange, please do not be alarmed; I shall be perfectly alright.' He closed his eyes and frowned in concentration.

'Even after all these years, I can see it all so clearly. There are six of us in the crew room and two more sitting outside, pondering over a chess board. There's music in the background – Glenn Miller's 'Elmer's Tune'. The walls are covered in pin-ups, photos of the squadron, past and present, and aircraft recognition posters with their silhouettes of German aircraft. The room is sparsely furnished with a few tables and some rickety folding chairs and a couple of battered old armchairs, pride of place being reserved for the bar which stood immediately opposite the entrance. It had a red and white striped awning, surmounted by the squadron crest, a blazing arrow with the motto, *Swift and true*. The bar itself is decorated with cut-outs of Walt Disney characters.'

It was noticeable that Clive had been talking in a mixture of past and present tenses almost as if there were times when he was actually there, describing the scene as he saw it. As he spoke, too, it became evident that he was slipping into a trance. His head began to sink forward until his chin was resting on his chest, his breathing deepened and, for a while it seemed as if he had fallen into a deep sleep. The audience stirred restlessly. Suddenly he spoke, and this time the mixture of tenses disappeared and he spoke entirely in the present.

'At the moment, the counter is strewn with coffee cups and ashtrays full of dog-eared cigarette ends. A thin blue smoke haze, slowly undulating, hangs like strata about 3 feet above the floor. Outside, the late summer sun is shining warmly and somewhere, in the nearby fields, a lark is singing its heart out.

'Much to my consternation, I find that George Reynolds is as interested in me as I am in him. He rubs his eyes and stares at me again and for a few moments, we just stand there eyeballing each other. Then, as if by mutual consent, we simultaneously avert our eyes, both of us having the grace to look embarrassed.

'I cast a swift glance at my companions. Their faces remain impassive; nothing there to suggest that they have seen anything unusual. So why the heck am I the only one to witness this phenomenon? I stagger to an armchair and flop into it gratefully, wondering if I'm losing my marbles. Dick Jenkins is speaking.

' "I hope you will forgive this intrusion, gentlemen, but Mr Reynolds here has expressed a desire to be shown around the dispersal. He is, I can assure you, a very special case."

'George Reynolds speaks then and his words echo hollowly as if he were talking through the end of a very long pipe. Again, the others show no signs of having noticed anything unusual and I begin to suspect the first symptoms of battle fatigue.

' "I would appreciate it, gentlemen, if you would allow me to stroll around the dispersal and witness the general squadron activities. You see, I too was a part of this scene 38 years ago and for as long as I am able, I would like to be a part of it again."

'Now it is my companion's turn to look astonished. Skipper starts to say something but Dick Jenkins holds up his hand and stops him.

' "I know what you're going to say, David; I said it to myself not a half hour since. How could he be part of this scene 38 years ago? For one thing" (he gives George Reynolds a close scrutiny), "in my office he looked fortyish; now look at him! I wouldn't put his age at much past 25. At either age the whole thing is impossible. If we go back 38 years from now, that brings us to 1902. There was no scene comparable to this in that year. It wasn't until December 17th of the following year that the Wright Brothers flew their first powered aircraft. And so," he eyes us significantly, "the words only make sense if spoken by someone returning to 1940 from 1978 – 38 years from now!"

'This statement elicits five incredulous gasps – not from me, I believe him – which develop into gales of laughter.

' "Pull the other one, Dick," chuckles Skip. "April Fools' Day has come and gone."

'Chippy Woods leans weakly against the bar and wipes his streaming eyes.

' "Oh, I say, that's rich. Chaps, meet Mr 1978, the future we're fighting for."

' "If he's an example," says Ginger Bennett, eyeing George disdainfully, "I suggest we surrender immediately."

'Alan West has laughed so much he is overcome by a debilitating bout of hiccups and is hicking quietly in between chuckles.

'By now, we have been joined by the two chess players who want to know if this is a private party or can anyone join in. No-one seems inclined to enlighten them as to the cause of the hilarity, so they decide to remain and pick up the threads as they go along.

'Throughout this ribaldry, George Reynolds just sits and grins amiably at the mickey takers. Dick Jenkins' scarred face is twisted in an impassive smile. In the face of this attitude of self-assurance, the chuckles gradually subside. Soon the silence is broken only by an occasional 'hic' from Alan.

'Skipper frowns. "By God, Dick, you're not really serious about this are you? You can't honestly expect us to believe that . . . that . . . ?" Incredulity renders him speechless.

'Dick gives Skip a sympathetic smile and leads him, slightly dazed, to the nearest chair.

' "Sit down, David, you too Mr Reynolds. I can see that I'm going to have to do some explaining."

'Someone says, "This had better be good," and not to be left out, I join the others clustered around the table.

'George Reynolds looks at me and grins. Despite myself I return his grin and a kind of affinity is established between us. I notice, too, at the same time, that he now looks 5 years younger and is not quite as distinct as he was 10 minutes ago.

'Dick Jenkins pulls an envelope out of his pocket and empties the contents onto the table: some money (notes and coins), what looks like an identity card and another document wrapped in some sort of transparent material. He picks up one of the notes and gives it to Skip.

' "Now, David, tell me, have you ever seen anything like that before?"

'Skip examines it closely, front and back, and then holds it up to the light.

' "It says it's a pound note," he says, shaking his head in bewilderment, "but it's not like any pound note I've ever seen. For one thing, it's smaller and the colour's different." He examines it again. "Picture of Sir Isaac Newton 1642–1727 on the back." He turns the note over. "A portrait of some dame wearing a coronet on the front. Says up the top *Bank of England* and underneath the words *I promise to pay the bearer on demand the sum of one pound* – that I recognise. It has a serial number, but only on the bottom right-hand corner." He looks at Dick.

' "What is it, a new type of pound note to fool the enemy? And who's the doll?"

'The grin climbs higher up the right side of Dick Jenkins' face. The old rascal is enjoying himself. "Just to the right of the lady's left shoulder there are some letters. Read them, David."

'Skip squints at the note. "There's an *E*, then a very small Roman *II*, followed by an *R*. He slowly repeats the combination. Suddenly, his face clears and he gasps in astonishment. "It's a royal cipher." His voice drops into an awed whisper. "I thought her face looked vaguely familiar. It's princess Elizabeth isn't it, only here she's Queen Elizabeth the second? My God, it's true," the note drops from his nerveless fingers, "he *is* from the future!" He becomes terribly excited.

' "Dick, do you realise what we have here? This will be worth a fortune; every newspaper in the country will be falling over themselves to get their hands on this story." He walks over to where George is sitting and subjects him to a detailed study. He turns and glances at Dick.

' "How old did you say he was?"

'Dick laughs bitterly. "That's the rub, he's getting progressively younger. An hour ago, in my office, he looked about forty; 15 minutes ago about 25; now look at him? How old would you say he was, 18–20? The process seems to begin slowly and accelerates with the passage of time." He looks moodily at George, who, to my eyes, is becoming increasingly indistinct. "At this rate, he'll be a baby in an hour, and then what? Does he become an egg and disappear in a puff of smoke?" George is still smiling benignly and seems in no way perturbed by Dick's gloomy forecast.

'Dick is about to say something but his words are drowned in the deafening clamour of the alarm bell. Instinctively, I glance at my watch, it is 10.32. A flustered corporal pokes his nose around the door and gasps, "Forty bandits plus, sir, almost on top of us. 12000 feet,"

'Skip hurtles to his feet, knocking his chair flying. "Right chaps, scramble. Rendezvous over the airfield, Angels one five." He grabs hold of me as I shoot past him. "No, not you, Clive. I want you to keep an eye on Mr Reynolds, don't let him out of your sight."

'He looks at Dick and smiles. "Do you still want to go?"

'Dick's chair goes over with a crash as he leaps to his feet. "Do I . . . ? You can bet your sweet life I do." His face is radiant. "Thanks David, I'll not forget this." Skip gives him an amiable grin. "You'll be cursing me 5 minutes from now. Get yourself into a flying suit and take Clive's kite, I'm sure he won't mind." He grins at me, winks and shouts "Good luck," as he hurtles through the door. I'm thinking he's going to get the book thrown at him if ever Bailey gets to hear about this.

'Dick is struggling into his flying suit. I turn to speak to George Reynolds. He's not there. Blast his hide, probably gone outside to witness the scramble. Dick runs past me shouting, "Thanks Clive." I hear the crash and roar of the first Spit starting up. Now there's confusion everywhere. I run outside. A flight sergeant is yelling at everyone to get down the shelters. I

59

hear the vicious whine of a Stuka, and glance upwards to see it pull out of its dive, a bomb hurtling earthwards. I see it burst and feel the stunning concussion. More explosions and the harsh clatter of cannon fire. There is a powerful punch in my back, the earth reels and rushes up to meet me . . .'

Clive's voice trailed away into a whisper and for a good minute he continued to stare sightlessly into space. Then he blinked, drew the back of his hand across his eyes and turned to Miss Beresford.

'I guess I did it again, eh, Dorothy?'

She beamed at him. 'Oh, you dear man, what a perfect subject you are. This is going to be easy. What time is it?'

Clive glanced at his watch. 'Nine fifty eight.'

She nodded her satisfaction. 'Good, we have almost 30 minutes.' She looked down on the villagers and smiled at the stupefied expression on their faces. They had not yet recovered from Clive's narrative or the strange transformation he had undergone in front of their eyes.

The vicar was the first to recover. For some time he had been exhibiting signs of extreme agitation, now he could contain himself no longer. He jumped to his feet, glared at Miss Beresford and banged the table in anger.

'For God's sake, Miss Beresford, What ye're doing is evil, 'tis the work of the devil himself.' His voice rose pleadingly. 'Stop it, I beg of you, stop it before ye unleash forces over which we have no control.'

The vicar's fear swept through the hall like a contagion. Feet shuffled uneasily and Albert Brewster put voice to their fears.

'Perhaps the vicar's right, Miss Beresford. Much as we would like to be rid of these ghosts, perhaps it would be better if we left things as they are.'

A chorus of assent greeted his remarks and Dorothy Beresford sprang to her feet and leant on the table, her knuckles gleaming white under the tightly stretched skin. She glared at the villagers.

'So you want to stop, eh? You think you can go on living the way you have all these years, rubbing shoulders with your

60

friendly neighbourhood ghosts; perhaps even sharing the occasional pint with them at the Redford Arms. You fools,' she sneered scornfully, 'don't you realise that it can never be that way again. After today, all of you . . . the sweep of her arm encompassed the cowering villagers . . . all of you will be in mortal danger.' She remained on her feet long enough for the warning to sink in, then sat down.

Clive Prescott leaned towards her and said something *sotto voce* to which she responded with a nod. She stood up again.

His lordship's gavel banged the table once more, nipping the rising buzz of conversation in the bud. Dorothy smiled her thanks.

'Wing Commander Prescott and I have agreed,' she told the villagers, 'that it's time you knew some more about the facts behind these manifestations. Firstly, then, you must know that the person responsible for them – although he doesn't know it – is at this moment in the intensive care unit at the East Sussex hospital. His name is George Reynolds – the one to whom the wing commander referred – and he is there as a result of an accident which occurred near here in the early hours of this morning.'

'They know about the accident, Dorothy,' Clive intervened, 'young Andrew there found him.' He indicated Andrew with a nod.

'Very well. Then I must tell you that George Reynolds is in a deep coma after having clinically died during the operation. Now, during my investigations into psychic phenomena, I have, time and again, come across cases where it would appear that the spirit has prematurely left the body. This condition is known as autoscapy or transcendence. In such cases the patient appears to die, is revived artificially but remains in a comatose condition until such time as the spirit either returns to the body, in which case, the patient begins a slow recovery, or fails to return, in which case, the patient dies and the spirit remains earthbound. This unfortunate spirit, finding itself marooned in time and space, begins to cast about for an affinity with which to associate. Now, it is well known that all life forms possess individual auras and, unless the spirit is marooned at a time when its physical counterpart exists, it can never find a life form with which it is truly compatible, so it compromises and merges with the nearest it can find. This poor creature – and it could be an animal – immediately becomes 'possessed' as the ancients called it, the degree of 'possession' depending upon the extent of compatibility and rejection of the host body.' She glanced at her watch and hurried on.

'Those who are lucky enough to find themselves in a period in which their physical counterpart exists, begin a process of metamorphosis which terminates when the spirit aura exactly matches that of its counterpart. This is the perfect affinity and its merger with the host body produces no ill effects or rejection.

'Now, each of these spirits possesses an area of influence, the extent of which I have, so far, been unable to define, but one of the effects of this influence is to hold earthbound the spirit of anyone dying within its radius. The only way that these spirits can find release is to remove the force that is holding them earthbound.'

'When George Reynolds crashed, his spirit returned to 1940,' she gave an expressive shrug, 'why, I don't know. Maybe he has a special affinity with that year, maybe it was pure accident, but, mark the date, ladies and gentlemen. Today is September the 15th, the 38th anniversary of that tragic day when RAF Lynton Down was practically wiped off the face of the map, a day in which the ghosts of the dead, held earthbound by the spirit of George Reynolds, relive those fatal hours, beginning with his accident and terminating when his spirit successfully accomplishes the merger with his physical body. This process has been repeated for 38 years, but it is only now that something can be done about it. We have reached the actual date of the accident and it should be possible to put an end to this constant renewal by stopping the association of George Reynolds with his younger physical body. If that can be accomplished, and if George Reynolds in hospital still lives, the spirit will have no recourse but to return to the body it has prematurely vacated.' Dorothy paused and gazed down earnestly at the spellbound audience.

'It is imperative that this is done quickly or George Reynolds will die before it can be accomplished, and there is another reason for haste. As the time draws near to the actual date from which George's spirit was precipitated, those earthbound spirits become progressively malignant, their spheres of influence spreading outward from the centre of the vortex – in this case, the RAF station – and reaching their peak on the instant of the release of the holding spirit. Then, those "harmless" little encounters that you have previously experienced will become moments of sheer terror where any physical contact with the spirit will result in instant death.' Her final words were accompanied by a swift chopping motion of her right hand. For a moment she stood gazing down on the villagers, breathing heavily with the passion of her warning, then she slumped in the chair, physically exhausted. Clive Prescott took her hand in his, gave it a reassuring squeeze and whispered 'Good girl, that'll give 'em something to think about.'

Lord Redford humphed and ran a finger under his collar, suddenly finding it uncomfortably tight. He gave Dorothy a quick, nervous smile.

'You have a positive genius for making the blood curdle, Miss Beresford, and, but for the fact that Andrew Stockton has already experienced a close encounter with this new form of malignancy, I would dismiss your words as pure conjecture.'

Dorothy's eyes scanned the audience, 'You have someone here who has seen the malignants?' she asked, excitedly. 'Who is he? Point him out to me.'

'If you remember, Miss Beresford, he is the lad who discovered George Reynolds' body.' Lord Redford peered into the audience. 'Stand up, Andrew, tell Miss Beresford exactly what happened after you found the body.'

Andrew shuffled to his feet and repeated almost word for word, with perhaps a minor embellishment here and there and an occasional emphasis for effect, the story of his terrifying experience.

'Dorothy's joy knew no bounds. Her eyes sparkled and she clasped her hands ecstatically. 'Proof at last. Oh, Andrew, you don't know what this means to me. Thank you, thank you.' Andrew smiled indulgently and sat down.

Ralph Morgan's voice rose plaintively from the audience. 'Then will someone please tell me what the blazes it was I saw in the old guardroom?'

Dorothy cast an anxious glance at the speaker and turned to Lord Redford for enlightenment. He, in turn, puffed out his cheeks and glared resentfully at his gamekeeper.

'I begin to wish that you had arrived a little earlier, Miss Beresford. Having to listen to all these repeats is most trying.'

Dorothy smiled sympathetically. 'I understand, your lordship, but if it doesn't take too long, I would like to know what it was this gentleman saw. You never know, it might have a direct bearing on the situation.'

'Oh, all right, then,' said his lordship, petulantly. 'Tell her, Ralph, but for pity's sake keep it short, there's a good chap.'

As Ralph progressed through his description of the mutilated, blood-soaked spectre that had suddenly confronted him, Dorothy's face cleared and, towards the end of the narrative, she was smiling.

'Thank you, Ralph. What you saw – and it must have been a truly terrifying sight – was probably the newly released spirit of George Reynolds. It is most unusual for living people to witness such things. Tell me, Ralph, are you clairvoyant?'

He laughed. 'Not that I know of, miss.'

Dorothy pursed her lips thoughtfully. 'I wouldn't mind betting that you are, Ralph. Being a living person, you would see the spirit in exactly the same condition as its host body at the moment of vacation; which accounts for its gory appearance. On the other hand, the spirit world would notice nothing unusual and would accept him as one of them.'

She turned to the Revd Sinclair. 'Do you still think we are doing the devil's work, Mr Sinclair?'

The reverend gentleman studied her over the rim of his glasses. 'I still believe there is devil's work being done here, Miss Beresford,' he said, gravely, 'but I don't think it's any of your doing, and if I can play a part in whatever course of action you are about to take, I shall be only too pleased to offer my contribution, no matter how small.'

'Thank you, reverend. Do you know anything about exorcism?'

Revd Sinclair looked flustered. 'My goodness, is that what you have in mind? I know a little but not enough, I'm sure, to exorcise this lot.' That last remark provoked a ripple of laughter and Dorothy hastened to reassure him.

'Only if what we are about to attempt fails, Mr Sinclair, will we call upon your services.'

'Miss Beresford.' Lord Redford, not always the most patient of men, could contain himself no longer. 'Would you please get to the point and tell us what the blue blazes it is you are about to attempt?'

Dorothy smiled at him disarmingly. 'My apologies, Lord Redford, I will indeed come to the point as you say, but first bear with me a moment longer while I tell you all a little about Clive Prescott.'

'A little over 5 years ago he wrote to me at the Institute telling of a recurring dream he had been having for some time. The nature of this dream was such as to arouse my curiosity and I immediately arranged a meeting with him. I drove up to the market town of East Dereham, near where he was currently stationed, and over dinner at the George Hotel he told me more of his dream, the essence of which was the events occurring at RAF Lynton Down on the morning of September 15th 1940. You already know the details; Clive has just described them to you. But it was his manner when he was relating the dream that intrigued me. As you have already witnessed, he begins normally enough and then as time goes on he gradually becomes part of the dream, describing the events as if he were actually there. He has total recall. We had many sessions together and I taped numerous recordings of the interviews.' She smiled at Clive. 'You should have seen the shocked look on his face when I played back the first recording. To cut a long story short, I persuaded him to take up residence here in the village when his term of service expired and wait for the crucial date, September 15th 1978 – today. I don't know whether I

65

expected that ring on the telephone this morning or not but, when it came, I was ready. Now,' her manner became at once brisk and businesslike, 'I'll tell you what I am about to attempt. As you know, when Clive describes his dream it as if he were actually there on the spot. But he's not – not quite. He needs just that extra little push to put him there and I am going to attempt to give him just that.'

# Chapter 7

'Sit down, Cpl. Miller.' Sqn. Ldr. Jenkins nodded at a vacant chair. 'I want you to take notes of my conversation with Mr Reynolds.'

Judy Miller cast a cursory glance at George and sat herself primly on the edge of the chair, her note pad and pencil at the ready.

Sqn. Ldr. Jenkins seemed in no hurry to begin the conversation. He leant back in his chair, pursed his lips and tapped out a slow, monotonous beat on his desk with the tip of one finger, never once taking his eyes off George's face. He held that stance until the cough of a Spitfire starting up interrupted his thoughts. A second Merlin spluttered, caught and added its throaty roar to the first. It was immediately followed by another until the air vibrated to the synchronous roar of aircraft engines. He pushed his chair back and crossed over to the window.

'Come over here, Mr Reynolds, I'd like you to see this,' he said, without turning. George joined him in time to see three Spitfires rise above the trees bordering the airfield. They banked as one and swept over the station, passing low over SHQ. The sound of their engines could still be heard as the second trio flashed overhead. This process was repeated time and again, the engines of each succeeding wave renewing the diminishing roar of their predecessors, until George had counted 42 aircraft. Not until the sound of the last engines had died away into the distance did Sqn. Ldr. Jenkins turn from the window with a sigh and resume his seat. George did likewise.

'Those two squadrons are off to reinforce Biggin Hill and Hornchurch. That leaves us with just one squadron, Mr Reynolds, to patrol the whole southern sector. Heaven help us if Jerry decides to pay us a little visit now.' He glanced at Judy, busy scribbling away, and waved his hand. 'That's off the record, Cpl Miler.' Judy nodded and rubbed out the offending words.

'And now, Mr Reynolds,' Sqn. Ldr. Jenkins reached for the envelope. 'let's open this "Pandora's Box" and see what comes out, shall we?' He slit open the envelope and shook the contents onto the desk.

'Well now, what have we here?' He picked up a pound note and subjected it to close scrutiny, turning it over and holding it up to the light. Something caught his eye and he peered at it closely. He opened his desk drawer, extracted a magnifying glass and examined it through the lens. His brow creased in a puzzled frown and he looked up at George.

'You are more of an enigma than I imagined, Mr Reynolds.' He held up the note between finger and thumb. 'Is it possible that you can explain this to my satisfaction?'

George grinned. Apart from Judy's disturbing presence (and he would have to do something about that) he was actually beginning to enjoy himself.

'I think so.'

'Well, then,' Sqn. Ldr. Jenkins settled himself comfortably in his chair and crossed his legs, 'by all means fire away, you have my undivided attention.'

'Before I begin, I have one stipulation to make.'

'And that is?'

'That what I am about to tell you will be for your ears alone.'

'Sorry, Mr Reynolds, no can do.' The shake of his head was final.

'Very well, then I say nothing.' George sat back in his chair and regarded the officer impassively.

Sqn. Ldr. Jenkins sighed regretfully. 'Then it will have to be the hard way.'

'Not necessarily. Those coins you have there, examine them and especially mark the dates. Do not repeat them, just look.'

The officer looked nonchalantly at the assortment of coins in front of him then he suddenly stiffened, reached forward and picked up a 10p piece. For almost a minute he studied the coin, turning it first one way and then the other, then he set it aside and shuffled through the remaining coins this time choosing a 5p piece. After a moment's examination, he replaced it and looked at George with something approaching awe. For the first time, he seemed at a loss for words.

'I – I don't understand, where . . .' His voice trailed away into silence as he gazed in fascination at the little array of coins.

George sensed that he was now in command of the situation and he lost no time in taking advantage of it.

'Those are my *bona fides*, squadron leader. They, together with my driving licence and identity card, if you care to examine them also, should prove to you that I am . . .' He cut himself short, remembering Judy's presence just in time. He glanced at her. She, too, was looking curiously at the coins, but being too far away from the desk to notice details, she was wondering what all the fuss was about. George thanked his lucky stars that there were no 50p pieces among them.

He rose from the chair, took a couple of quick paces and faced the squadron leader.

'Now look. In order to prove to you that I am who I say I am, it will be necessary for me to broach certain . . . ah . . . delicate matters, subjects affecting the course of the war; and, while not doubting Cpl. Miller's integrity for one minute,' he smiled at Judy, 'for personal reasons, I would prefer to discuss them with you alone.'

For some moments Sqn. Ldr. Jenkins stared at the coins, seemingly unable to take his eyes off them, then he slowly and deliberately stubbed his cigarette out in the tray.

'All right, Mr Reynolds,' he said, quietly, gazing at the crushed cigarette, 'it shall be as you wish. Cpl. Miller,' he smiled at Judy, 'would you leave us, please. I'll call you if I need you.'

'Yes sir.' Judy stood up, closed her note pad, shot George an unfriendly look and left the room with as much dignity as her hurt feminine pride could muster. As the door closed behind her, George whispered, 'Goodbye Judy.' There was still a lump in his throat as he stubbed out his cigarette and returned to his chair.

At that very moment, 27 JU 87s of Hauptmann von Brau-
chitsch's 4th Wing Lehrgeschwader 1 were rising from Tramec-
ourt airfield in France to rendezvous over the channel with 15
ME 109s of Hauptmann Scholtz's 3rd Wing, 54th Fighter
Group, based at Guines. Their target? The almost undefended
RAF Lynton Down.

# Chapter 8

'And now, Mr Reynolds,' the squadron leader began, when a click and a crackle of static from the Tannoy interrupted his words.

'Stand by for broadcast.' There was a brief pause, then the voice continued. 'A general meeting will be held in the station cinema at ten hundred hours today. All personnel not on essential duty are to attend. End of broadcast.' A further click, then the telephone shrilled. With a tut of annoyance Sqn. Ldr. Jenkins picked up the receiver.

'Yes, sir, I heard it.' He glanced at George. 'He's with me now, sir.' The earpiece squawked. 'Hard to tell, sir; about an hour maybe.' There followed a further prolonged bout of squawking, during which he suddenly sat bolt upright and became increasingly agitated.

'But sir,' he protested, 'with respect, surely that would further inflame an already delicate situation.' He winced and held the receiver away from his ear as the squawking reached an unbearable pitch. When it had subsided he said reluctantly, 'Very well, sir, I'll inform Security.' He replaced the receiver and stared at it as if doubting its very existence.

'The man's mad, absolutely stark staring bonkers. Can you imagine it?' he turned to George, his voice rising with incredulity. 'With the entire station on the verge of mutiny, he has to aggravate things by sealing off the camp, cancelling all leave and posting armed guards around the cinema during the meeting. Wartime or no, the men won't stand for it; there'll be a hell of a bust up, but what can I do?' He threw up his arms in a gesture of despair. 'Apart from having him certified and taking over command of the station, there is absolutely nothing that can be done.'

'What about the AOC, shouldn't he be informed?' asked George.

Sqn. Ldr. Jenkins shook his head vigorously. 'Group Captain Bailey is my commanding officer, I couldn't go over his head.'

George shrugged. 'Then you will just have to do as he says and wait for the explosion.'

'Perhaps you're right.' His eyes gleamed and a crafty smile tugged at the corners of his mouth. 'Yes, Mr Reynolds, maybe you have something there. If there was a bust up, there'd be an investigation. People in high places would want to know why such a serious situation had been allowed to develop. An awful lot of dirty linen would be washed and most of it Group Captain Bailey's. It might be a drastic cure, but it's probably the only way we're going to rid ourselves of this martinet.'

Satisfied that he had made the right decision, he reached for the phone.

'Extension 252 please.' He grinned at George. 'Whoever allocated that number to Security must have had a sense of humour.' George returned the grin, remembering the number of occasions he had had his various misdemeanours recorded on charge form 252.

The telephone gave forth a solitary 'ting'. 'Hello Phil, Dick Jenkins here. Orders from God. He wants the station sealed off, no one goes out or comes in . . .' Once again he winced and held the receiver away from his ear as a minor explosion occurred within the earpiece. 'Yes, yes I know, take it easy will you, Phil, this ear's already had one battering today. Now, listen, that's not all . . .' The earpiece rumbled ominously. 'He wants you to post armed guards around the cinema during the meeting.' He quickly removed the telephone away from his ear in anticipation of the inevitable outburst, but only a shocked silence ensued. Tentatively, he replaced the receiver to his ear. 'Are you there, Phil? Right, now no arguments, there's a good chap, just do it. Issue rifles but no ammunition, is that understood? Good, now listen. An awful lot of shit is going to fly, but if we play our cards right we'll get rid of Bailey and come up smelling of roses, OK? Right, oh, and Phil; inform the SWO will you? I think he should know what's going on.' He replaced the receiver and stared at it moodily.

'All I've done is to carry out a legal order and yet, do you know Mr Reynolds,' he cocked an eye at George, 'I feel like a bloody conspirator.'

'That's hardly surprising, squadron leader,' George answered, sympathetically, 'considering the provocative nature of the order and the inevitable consequences of obeying it.' Despite himself, George was beginning to have a wholesome respect for this officer, even liking him; nevertheless, he continued to be on his guard; after all, the man did have a somewhat unpleasant reputation.

'Hmm.' Sqn. Ldr. Jenkins reflected on this for a moment, then shrugged away his thoughts and devoted his full attention to the problem of George and the Suspicious Currency.

'And now, Mr Reynolds, perhaps you will be so good as to explain how this . . . ah . . . currency,' he waved a nonchalant hand at the scatter of coins and notes on his desk, 'came to be in your possession.'

'Delighted.' George's lips twitched at the thought of the preposterous tale he was about to spin. He was reasonably confident of the outcome, for was it not true that the more preposterous a tale, the more likely it is to be believed? And had he not certain proofs to offer? He felt a little sorry for the officer, who was about to become a very confused and perplexed man.

'To begin with,' he picked up a 10p piece and held the edges between finger and thumb, 'as you will observe, this is not a two shilling piece.' He turned the coin so that the 'tails' side faced the officer. 'It is a decimal coin and worth 10 new pence or 2.4 shillings in the old currency.' He rotated the coin through 180 degrees with the tip of his finger. 'The head is that of Queen Elizabeth II – Princess Elizabeth as she is now – and the date,' he squinted at the coin, 'is 1976.' Sqd. Ldr. Jenkins' eyes narrowed a fraction and his lips compressed in a visible effort to remain silent.

George selected another coin and pushed it towards the officer, who stared at it impassively. 'This is one with which you will be more familiar. As you can see, it's a two shilling piece; the head is that of the present king, but the date is 1951. We still use these coins, together with the shilling as 5 and 10 pence pieces. There is also a seven-sided coin worth 50 pence – your 10 shillings – and, as you will have noticed, the pound note is smaller and worth 100 new pence.' He picked up his driving licence and RAFVR identity card and dropped them in front of the officer.

'Examine those, if you will.' His eyes followed the officer's hand as he picked up the documents. 'You will observe that one is a driving licence of a type unfamiliar to you and the other is an RAFVR identity card which will tell you that I hold the rank of Squadron Leader. Now, look at the date of birth.' He grinned as the officer's jaw dropped as he tried to reconcile the date with the professed age of the man facing him. His eyes slowly rose to fix George with a stare of blank incredulity. George's grin widened.

'Confusing, isn't it?'

Sqn. Ldr. Jenkins suddenly realised that his mouth was wide open and closed it with a snap. He swallowed nervously and looked at George as if he were a primed bomb, about to explode at any moment.

'Sgt. Hawkins was right. There *is* more to you than meets the eye. In God's name, man, who are you? Where do you come from?' The words came softly at first, then more strongly accompanied by an indefinable emotion. What was it? Fear? Awe? George couldn't be certain. Whatever it was, it gave him an impression of ascendency; of being in complete charge and, because of this, his answer was perhaps a shade too flippant.

'I'd have thought that it would have been pretty obvious by now.'

The officer's reaction swiftly dispelled that attitude, restored the status quo and cleared up the mystery of the hidden emotion – it was anger. He brought his fist down on the desk with a crash that rattled the phone in its cradle, collapsed the little pile of coins and made George jump.

'The only thing that's obvious at the moment, Mr Reynolds, is the fact that you are in deep trouble and, if I don't get some

74

satisfactory answers from you soon, I shall make it my personal business to see that you face a firing squad within a week. All I've heard from you so far are innuendoes and hints; all based on a collection of coins and documents, which for all I know could be forgeries, although to what purpose I can't for the life of me imagine. I need proof, Mr Reynolds, proof that you were born in 1922, are 56 years of age and have somehow returned to 1940 from 1978. As I've said before, Mr Reynolds, I don't like loose ends and this situation has so many, it's positively dis-integrating. It has all the hallmarks of a first class nightmare and I want you to convince me that I'm not dreaming.' He glanced at his watch. 'And I'll give you a half hour to do it in.'

He helped himself to another cigarette and gestured to George to do the same. As George bent to accept the proferred light, he could almost feel the officer's eyes doing an effective trepanning job to the top of his skull. They were still drilling away at his face as he gratefully inhaled a soothing lungful of smoke. He held it there for a moment, then exhaled slowly as he tried to assemble his scattered thoughts.

Things were not going quite as he had anticipated. Somehow he had to regain the initiative and the only way to do that was to prove he was who he said he was – which was going to be difficult, considering he wasn't – or, at least, up to a point he wasn't. He was still George Reynolds and, whether he had been hurled back to 1940 by a time machine or via a fatal accident in the form of a disembodied spirit, really made no difference. He was here and could only explain his presence by one of those two alternatives. In order to convince the officer that he had arrived by means of the latter alternative, he had to prove to him that he also was dead. George's mind boggled at the thought. So it would have to be the former. He began by asking a question.

'Tell me, squadron leader, what do you think would be a man's reaction if he were to be suddenly transported from 1902 to the present day?'

'I should imagine he would be speechless with amazement.'

'Exactly. 1940 with its miracles of modern science would be as alien to him as 1978 would be to you.' George drew on his cigarette and as he leaned forward to dispose of the ash, he scanned the officer's face for some kind of reaction. But, apart from the eyes briefly leaving George's face to rest momentarily on the coins, he betrayed not the faintest hint of emotion; except perhaps for the smile – an enigmatic Mona Lisa type smile, which may or may not have been a part of his natural expression, but which, nevertheless, left George with an uneasy cat and mouse type feeling. He cleared his throat.

'Science hasn't stagnated. In 1978, man has walked on the moon and spaceships have visited many of the planets of the solar system. We fly at more than twice the speed of sound so it is possible to breakfast in London and arrive in New York in time for another.'

Ah – that elicited a reaction. One eyebrow raised itself fractionally.

'The devil you say, twice the speed of sound, eh?'

'More,' George emphasised.

The officer seemed to be suitably impressed and, George hurried on to press home his advantage.

'A good many of the scientific marvels of 1978 will have been invented and developed during this war, some are yet to come, some you may already know about; the ENIGMA encoding machine for instance.' George paused again for some reaction, but none came so he pressed on. 'It was captured from the Germans and the only way to solve its millions of combinations was to build an electronic calculating machine. This formed the basis of our modern computers. Or perhaps you've heard of the jet engine or RADAR maybe?'

The officer jumped as if stung.

'Mr Reynolds, that information is highly classified.' He glanced nervously at the intercom keys. Satisfied that they were all in the off position, he glared at George.

'How do you know about these things?'

'I keep trying to tell you, squadron leader,' George said, patiently. 'I am a time traveller; I come from 1978. This war has been over for 33 years and most of your classified information is now common knowledge. Later on I will make a few predictions, but for the moment, I want to tell you about something, recently developed, that has nothing at all to do with the war.'

'A time machine, Mr Reynolds?' Sqn. Ldr. Jenkins tried to inject an unbelieving sneer into the words but, deep down, he was becoming aware of a dawning suspicion that this fellow, impossible though it may seem, might, just might, be telling the truth.

'Exactly.' Sensing the officer's confusion, George felt a surge of elation. His story was being accepted, albeit reluctantly. It only required that final bit of proof to push him into total acceptance.

For his part, Sqn. Ldr. Jenkins, DSO, DFC, was undergoing a totally new and frustrating experience. His nicely cut and dried little world, in which everything had to have an explanation, was suddenly developing the most alarming and unstable cracks. He felt a mounting resentment against the fate that had picked him, of all people, to cope with this situation and particularly against this fellow, lolling so nonchalantly in his chair and grinning at him so inanely. His resentment boiled over into anger and with it came a perverse determination not to believe a thing George said unless and until he was given irrefutable proof which even he would have to accept. The facial scar stood out like a jagged white slash as he struggled to keep his voice calm.

'I have no intention of sitting here listening to science fiction mumbo-jumbo about time machines. You say you are from 1978. Right, give me proof, Mr Reynolds – convince me.'

George gave a short, bitter laugh. 'Easier said than done. However, if I have read the signs correctly, it will soon become self-evident. In the meantime, permit me to indulge in a few predictions.'

'The first – and, this you will be able to check in tomorrow's papers – is that today will be fought the greatest air battle of the war, in which the destruction of 175 enemy aircraft will be claimed, for the loss of thirty of ours. Actually,' George smiled, 'these figures were later found to be a little on the optimistic side and were duly amended, but that doesn't detract from the fact that today will go down in history as the turning point in the Battle of Britain. From today, Hitler will abandon all hopes of invading England and will turn his attention on Russia. Trampling all over their mutual non-aggression pact, he will invade that country on June 22nd 1941. He will get to within sight of the gates of Moscow before being driven back by a combination of the Russian winter and a strategic Red Army offensive.

'After a vicious and unprovoked attack on Pearl Harbour by the Japanese, on December 7th 1941 which crippled their Pacific fleet, America will, at long last, enter the war. In October 1942, General Montgomery will counterattack at El Alamein and eventually drive Rommel out of North Africa. 1943 will see the invasion of Sicily and Italy by the Allies, to be followed shortly after by the capitulation of Italy, who, let's face it, had no stomach for the war in the first place. The Germans, however, will occupy Italy and continue to resist the Allies' advance. Mussolini will meet his fate at the hands of a horde of Italian Communist patriots. Together with his mistress and two others, his mutilated body will hang upside down on public display, outside a garage in Milan.

'The second front will be launched on the 6th of June 1944. It will be known as *D day* and will be directed against the beaches of Normandy. In that year, Hitler will launch his new secret weapons against us. The V1 or Doodlebug, as it will be called, will be a flying bomb, ramp-launched and designed to drop out of the sky when its fuel is exhausted. The V2, which is destined to be the forerunner of our modern spaceships, is a rocket with a 2000 lb warhead. It will attain a height of 60 miles before falling back to earth. London and the South-east will take the brunt of the bombardment, but although they do considerable damage, they arrive too late to have any effect on the course of the war, which will come to an end on May 8th 1945, VE day. The war against Japan will drag on until August of that year when it will end dramatically with the dropping of two atom bombs, one on Hiroshima and one on Nagasaki, completely laying waste both cities.'

Sqn. Ldr. Jenkins was about to capitulate. He had made up his mind that no one could make such comprehensive predictions without having had prior knowledge or personal experience of the related events. And the prediction regarding the atom bombs – that had the ring of truth about it. Einstein had predicted its possibility and then, a few years ago, Lord Rutherford actually succeeded in splitting the atom. Yes it was indeed possible that the bomb would come to fruition during this war. But just in case Chummy was making up a few of those dates, he'd test his memory a little. He consulted his notes.

'Mr Reynolds, what date does America enter the war?'

'December 7th 1941,' came the prompt reply.

'And when will – er – *D day* be?'

'June 6th 1944,' equally promptly.

'Thank you, Mr Reynolds.' He threw the pencil onto the desk blotter and flopped back in his chair. His left eye began to twitch, as it always did in times of stress, and he automatically massaged the adjacent scar-damaged tissue.

He was convinced – had been for some time but had been too pig-headed to admit it. The funny part about it was that the predictions played only a small part in wearing down his resistance – they had merely tended to corroborate that which he had already begun to suspect. No, it was something much more intrinsic – it was the man himself.

For some time now, he had been struggling to dismiss an ever-growing conviction that the fellow was getting visibly younger. Now at the end of George's peroration, he could ignore it no longer. He had already remarked on George's youthful appearance and what had the fellow replied? Something about it being part of the process. He hadn't paid much attention to it then, but now the words took on a new significance. If he had looked forty then, he looked thirty now. His hair was thick, dark and curly. Gone was the slight puffiness under the eyes and the beginnings of a double chin. Gone, too, was the thick coarseness of middle age. The man who faced him now was two stones lighter with bright clear eyes and a firm, smooth skin.

At 10.02 a.m., a convoy of three cars moved away from the village hall, passed the rambling, ivy-covered *Redford Arms*, over a small humped-back bridge which forded the stream that ran through the Redford estate and up the narrow, winding hedge-lined lane that led to the A23.

The leading vehicle – a Range Rover, festooned with direction-finding aerials, and radar scanners, and crammed with electronic equipment – was driven by Dorothy Beresford. A Ford Escort, with Clive Prescott behind the wheel and Peter Redford as a passenger, followed at convoy distance, while, taking up the rear, an ancient Morris Minor, driven by the Revd James Sinclair, trailed a ribbon of blue smoke and emitted the occasional sharp crack of protest from the exhaust.

Five minutes later, the convoy turned off the A23 into the short access road and entered the old airfield, passing the shell of the guardroom on the left and the derelict SHQ on the right. Rounding the small island, the vehicles took the tree-lined avenue which ran between the officer's and sergeant's messes then turned left onto the road which ran parallel to the hangars and circled the airfield. Here, Clive's Escort assumed the lead and, after a short distance, turned off the road onto a cracked and weed-strewn path which opened up into a concrete circle with rusty iron rings embedded here and there and measuring about 100 ft in diameter. At the far end of the concrete circle and some 20 yards or so into the ploughed field which surrounded it, two square concrete foundations were all that remained of the huts of No. 2 Dispersal.

# Chapter 9

'Shall I continue,' asked George, somewhat unnecessarily, since he knew what the answer would be.

Sqn. Ldr. Jenkins stared at George in silent fascination, his spirits sinking lower by the moment. So it was true; this fellow really was the genuine article. But, what to do with him? that was the problem. For the first time in his life he was experiencing a feeling of inadequacy. His command of the situation was slowly slipping from his grasp and there was nothing he could do about it. He consoled himself with the thought that anyone else faced with the same situation would be equally at a loss, but there was something else, nothing tangible, nothing he could put his finger on, just a gut feeling – a sense of urgency, a nagging insistence that time was running out. It was as if a door to the future was slowly opening before him, beyond which lay an all-encompassing blackness, deep and silent, stretching out to eternity. He suppressed a shudder and fixed George with a reproachful look.

'Why, Mr Reynolds, with all of past history to choose from, did you have to select this particular era, particularly my little part of it?'

George smiled. 'It was not my intention to burden anyone with my presence. As you will recall, I was brought here forcibly, handcuffed and complaining bitterly.'

Sqn. Ldr. Jenkins wriggled uncomfortably. 'Yes, I regret that Mr Reynolds, but there was a certain amount of justification you will agree.'

Having gained control of the situation, George could afford to be magnanimous. 'Let's forget it, shall we?'

He stood up, walked over to the window and gazed with

affectionate nostalgia on an old familiar scene. Immediately opposite, in front of the guardroom, twelve men clad in blue overalls, webbing belts and gaiters, stood at ease and listened with varying expressions of boredom and disinterest, while an equally bored and uninterested sergeant read to them from a sheet of paper clipped to a piece of three-ply board. George, who had, regrettably, had experience of this sort of thing, recognised a defaulter's parade when he saw one and smiled. He felt a close affinity with an unfortunate sentry who, unsure of the compliment he was to give to a flight lieutenant, changed his mind halfway through a *butt salute* and gave him a *present arms*, almost dropping his rifle in the confusion. The officer smiled, returned the salute and headed for SHQ.

His wandering gaze focused on three airmen rounding the island, their forage caps perched at jaunty angles, their helmet-burdened side packs slapping heavily against their thighs. All three whistled and cast appreciative glances at a shapely passing WAAF who, in return, elevated her nose disdainfully and studiously ignored the amorous noises that followed her up the road. George grinned; 'You'll never get anywhere with her, lads,' he thought, 'she's officers only.'

It was a typical morning in the life of an air force station, a living, breathing entity, each with its own personality and human characteristics. There were good stations and bad ones, ones which made one welcome and instantly at home, others over which hung an air of discontent and depression, which manifested itself in the low morale of its personnel. This was such a station and George felt a surge of anger that one man could change a thing of beauty and harmony into one of spite and malevolence.

Suddenly he froze, his attention riveted on a convoy of three vehicles moving up the access road towards the station. He could have sworn that they had not been there a second ago; the road ran straight for at least 400 yards and he would have spotted them long before this. It was as if they had suddenly loomed out of a thick bank of fog. He gasped. Two things suddenly became apparent to him. One was the fact that nothing seemed to exist beyond the point where the vehicles had first appeared, only a milky white opaqueness. The station was, in fact, an island trapped in time and space. The second was the vehicles themselves. Fuzzy and insubstantial, colourless and reflecting no sunlight, they comprised a Ford Escort and a Morris Minor 1000 led by a Range Rover festooned with radar scanners, aerials and direction-finding equipment, all decidedly post–1940 period. Noiselessly they glided up to and passed through the lowered barrier, while the sentry continued to stand at ease outside his box, blissfully unaware of the phenomenon appearing under his very nose.

The convoy sliced through the rear rank of the defaulter's parade as it did the three laughing airmen. It correctly followed the contours of the traffic island and headed on a collision course with a lorry coming from the opposite direction. The three vehicles ploughed remorselessly through the lorry, which continued on its way, its driver conducting an animated and uninterrupted conversation with his co-driver.

A cyclist, emerging from a side road, entered the little convoy from the left in the vicinity of the Escort's radiator and emerged from it somewhere between the Morris Minor's front and rear seats. George continued to gaze speechlessly after the last vehicle long after it had been swallowed up by a bend in the road.

Sensing that something was amiss, Sqn. Ldr. Jenkins joined George at the window and looked out, trying to establish the cause of George's obvious amazement.

'What is it, Mr Reynolds? Is something wrong?' he asked, seeing nothing unusual in the little cameos being enacted outside.

George shook his head. 'I . . . er . . . oh, nothing. Just thought for a minute that I saw someone I once knew, that's all.' He rapidly changed the subject. 'I would like to see as much of the station as I can while there is still a little time left. Perhaps a visit to a squadron dispersal if it can be arranged. I promise I won't get in the way.'

Dick Jenkins was about to deliver a flat refusal when he suddenly found that he had solved the problem of whom to select as a confidant. Of course, David Sheldon and his crew, why hadn't he thought of it before? Between them, they ought to be able to come up with some workable solution to the George Reynolds problem. Instantly his gloomy thoughts evaporated and he positively beamed at George.

'But, of course, my dear fellow, I'll take you down there myself.' He walked briskly over to his desk and picked up the telephone. 'Shan't keep you a moment, Mr Reynolds,' he called over his shoulder; 'Ah, extension 323 please.' Almost immediately there was a click and a tinny 'Number 2 Dispersal, Sheldon here.'

'Oh, hello David, Dick Jenkins . . .' The voice at the other end interrupted him, 'Now, look here Dick, if it's about that other business . . .' This time it was the turn of Dick Jenkins to interrupt.

'No, David it's not about that. I'd like to drop in on you for a few moments if that is convenient;' he glanced at George obliquely, 'there's someone here I'd like you to meet.' The telephone squawked its assent. 'Good, see you in five minutes then.' He replaced the receiver and pushed down one of the buttons of the intercom.

'Yes sir,' Judy's voice came through with a metallic clarity.

'If I'm wanted, Cpl. Miller, I shall be at No. 2 Dispersal.'

'Very good, sir.'

He snapped off the switch, reached for his hat and transferred it from the rack to his head. Smiling, he indicated the door.

'Shall we go, Mr Reynolds?'

George suddenly remembered an old wartime catch phrase. He grinned.

'After you, Claude.'

'No, after you, Cecil,' Dick Jenkins responded with a laugh. George was still chuckling quietly to himself as he clambered into the Humber staff car with its drab camouflage and masked headlights.

They threaded their way carefully between the knots of airmen and WAAFs who, in company with other 'non-essential personnel' were converging in droves on the Astra cinema. A small queue was already beginning to form outside as they drove past the cinema and George could sense the tension in the air as angry glances were cast at a squad of armed airmen, drawn up in three ranks and facing them from across the road. A warrant officer of such generous proportions that George immediately knew him to be the station warrant officer, stood at ease in front of the squad, while a young officer, whom George took to be the 'Phil' of the phone conversation with Dick Jenkins, hovered inconspicuously in the background. The SWO drew the squad up to attention as the car passed and threw up a smart salute, to which Dick Jenkins responded with a curt nod. He gazed grimly into the rear view mirror.

'There, Mr Reynolds, is a situation ripe for mutiny.'

George didn't answer. He was looking at a poster advertising the film currently showing at the cinema. It was 'Northwest Passage', starring Spencer Tracy and Robert Young, and he was remembering the day he had first seen that poster and his subsequent strange and inexplicable behaviour.

He was a young airman then, within a week of completing an armourer's course at RAF Kirkham, eight miles from Blackpool. Right now, he was strolling down the Golden Mile, arm in arm with Jean, a Preston girl he had met at a station dance during the first week of his course. He could see the scene as vividly as if he were actually there.

It was a Saturday and the late afternoon sun shone warmly from a clear blue sky. He was uncomfortably hot in his blue serge uniform and he was using his forage cap as a fan as he gazed enviously at the bathers frolicking in the sparkling waters of the Irish Sea. They stopped and looked down over the green painted railings at the crowded beach. People sunbathed in deck chairs or stretched out on the warm, soft sand. Some with handkerchiefs knotted around their heads and trousers rolled up to the knee, paddled at the water's edge. A crowd of excited children clustered in front of a gaily coloured Punch and Judy stall, cheered and clapped each time Judy dealt Punch the traditional blow with her club. Further down the beach, a line of donkeys, each with its ears sticking out of a conical straw hat, patiently awaited their turn to transport yet another budding equestrian a few yards up the beach and back again.

'Wish I'd brought my bathing trunks, don't you?' said George heaving himself off the railings.

'Ee, I do that.' Jean had an attractive Lancashire accent. She slipped her arm through George's and they continued their stroll down the promenade.

A tram with its single deck open to the elements rumbled past and, in the distance, dominating the northern aspect, the slender latticework of Blackpool Tower rose majestically out of a line of buildings fronting the North Shore.

'Fancy going to the pictures?' said George, 'There's a choice between "Boy's from Cyracuse" with Alan Jones and Martha Raye or "Northwest Passage" with Spencer Tracy and Robert Young. I fancy the last one myself.'

'Me, too. I like Spencer Tracy and that Robert Young,' she closed her eyes in mock ecstasy, 'Ee, 'e's that dreamy.'

'That'll be enough of that, my girl,' said George, severely. 'You be content with what you've got.'

She squeezed his arm and rested her head on his shoulder. 'I am, I am.'

'OK, that's settled then. Race you to the tram stop.'

For George in the car, memory suddenly became reality. He was running; he felt the exhilaration of the chase and shared the happy burst of laughter as girl and boy slithered to a halt at the tram stop. He saw the approaching tram through the eyes of his younger self; felt the fresh, cool air caress his cheeks and ruffle his hair as the tram pulled away, bell clanging and wheels grinding on the rails. He felt the thrill of Jean's thighs pressing against his and revelled in the carnal thoughts it precipitated. Oh yes, it was good to be young again.

There was a small queue waiting for the cinema to open when they arrived and they joined it under a poster of Spencer Tracy as Captain Rogers, sporting a beard and dressed in green buck-skin with a Scotch bonnet and flanked by his rangers. The queue remained stationary and, uncharacteristically, George began to fret:

'Damn these queues,' he muttered savagely. 'Everywhere you go there's bloody queues.'

86

'It's only a little one,' said Jean consolingly, 'we'll soon be inside.'

But George refused to be mollified. He tore his arm away from Jean's restraining hand and strode up to the front of the queue. He ran up the steps, grasped the amber-coloured glass handles of the closed doors and began to shake them violently.

'Hey you, stop that. Get back in the queue.'

A magnificently attired commissionaire, his fat face pink with indignation, heaved his bulk at George and endeavoured to prize his hands away from the handles.

George swung on him. 'Take your hands off me, you officious little bastard. Get these bloody doors open.'

'George, for heaven's sake what's the matter with you?' Jean was behind George and pulling at his sleeve. 'Come back in the queue, please.'

'Yeah, do as yer girl friend tells yer,' a truculent voice growled at him from the front of the queue. " 'Op it".'

George slowly turned on this new adversary. 'You gonna make me, louse?'

The man's face went a deep purple. 'Why, you jumped up little pipsqueak.' He lunged at George, who sidestepped, bumping heavily into Jean. She screamed, lost her footing, tumbled down the steps and lay in a motionless heap on the pavement.

As the man flew past, George assisted him on his way with a size eight boot planted with great force and accuracy on his backside. He tripped, cannoned off a pillar and measured his length on the tiled mosaic floor. He made a slight movement, groaned then lay still, a trickle of blood oozing from a gash over his right eye.

By now, the fat commissionaire was screaming for all three emergency services and a few more beside. His frantic yells eventually attracted the attention of a couple of service policemen who had been hoping for a quiet afternoon's stroll along the front, sampling the sea breezes. That this was not to be became apparent as they raced up to the scene.

'What's the trouble?' one of them asked.

'It's 'im,' gasped the fat doorman, pointing a quivering finger at George. "e's gone mad.'

Certainly the evidence did seem to favour the doorman's last remark. Hair ruffled and face suffused with rage, George was crouching, fists clenched and belligerently inviting the male members of the queue to either individual or collective combat – he didn't care which. The two SPs exchanged glances and sighed.

'Oh, brother, Jock, do we get 'em?' one remarked.

Jock grinned. 'Yeah Jim, but it helps pass the time don' it? C'm on.'

After pausing to ask a group of people with Jean if she was OK and receiving nods of assent, they unslung their truncheons and advanced on George. The one called Jock tapped him on the shoulder with his truncheon.

'OK lad, you've had your fun; time to go home now.'

George turned slowly, still crouching. The sight of the two SPs, one using his truncheon to slap his leg, the other tapping the palm of his hand significantly, seemed to give him infinite pleasure. He was spoiling for a fight and these two beauties would satisfy that desire admirably. With a howl of delight he sprang at them and they all went down in a tangle of arms and legs.

George's knee bent sharply and found a soft, yielding groin. With a screech of pain, Jock rolled clear of the mêlée, retching, eyes rolling and writhing in agony. With one temporarily disposed of, George was able to devote his full attention to the remaining SP. He fought unscientifically, punching wildly, kicking and even butting when the opportunity presented itself. His one aim in life at that moment, was to get his hands around Jim's neck and squeeze.

On the other hand, his opponent was well-versed in the art of self defence and easily parried George's wild swings. But what George lacked in finesse, he made up in strength and, slowly but surely, he was getting the upper hand. They fought almost silently; the only sound coming from the two struggling men was the hissing intake of breath and the scraping of boots on the tiled cinema forecourt floor. Inch by inch, George's hands crept closer to Jim's throat. Sweat poured from his forehead and ran in rivulets down his nose and cheeks. His teeth bared in a wolf-like snarl and with a superhuman effort, which dragged a shuddering sob from between his clenched teeth, his clawed finger closed lovingly around Jim's throat. His thumbs pressed deeper and deeper into a spot just under the Adam's apple. Eyes bulging and the tip of his tongue just beginning to protrude through his teeth, Jim struggled desperately to free his throat of that vice-like grip, but it was to no avail. Gradually his struggles grew weaker, his eyes bulged, his face took on a purple hue and his tongue lolled out of a mouth open and gasping for air. In a moment his heart would give its final convulsive beat and Jim would be dead.

But George hadn't reckoned on Jock's recuperative powers. He had stopped retching and the pain was gradually receding. Now his brain was able to assimilate the information his eyes were sending it and they told him that his colleague was having the life choked out of him. He shook his head to clear away the last traces of fuzziness and, spotting his truncheon lying a few feet away, he crawled towards it. As his hands closed over the ribbed handle, he gazed scornfully on the horror-stricken queue, frozen into immobility. 'Cowardly bastards,' he muttered through clenched teeth. He stood up, slowly and painfully and, gritting his teeth, stumbled the few paces separating him from the struggling men. Jock then raised his truncheon and brought it down with all the force he could muster on a spot just above George's left ear. There was a sickening 'clunk' and George collapsed across Jim's inert form. A moment later Jock's eyes rolled upwards, his knees buckled, and he joined the other two on the floor.

# Chapter 10

'Mr Reynolds, Mr Reynolds. Are you alright?'

George blinked and stared at Dick Jenkins uncomprehendingly. Slowly he became aware of his surroundings. He was in a car. It was being driven by an officer and, at that moment, they were passing a large hangar on the right and a group of squat brick buildings with barred windows on the left. This wasn't Kirkham! Where the hell was it and how had he got here? He groaned and ran his fingers through his hair.

'Where am I?'

Dick Jenkins smothered an oath and stamped viciously on the brakes. The car screeched to an abrupt halt and George's head came into violent contact with the top of the windscreen.

'What the hell . . .' George cut short his howl of indignation when Dick Jenkins' face suddenly assumed a wonderful, comforting familiarity. So that's what had happened. Up until now, the events that occurred outside that cinema in Blackpool on that summer day in 1940, and which culminated in a 28-day stretch at Colchester, had been a complete blank, his only knowledge being that which he had pieced together by questioning those involved. He had remembered nothing from the time he had boarded the tram on the Golden Mile, until he awoke in a bed in Station Sick Quarters with a lump behind his ear the size of a duck's egg and a monumental headache.

He had repeated this until he was blue in the face, first to the Medical Officer then with many stammering apologies to the battle-scarred SPs who had been briefly detained in the same ward for observation. He had repeated it to a visiting 'shrink' who, nodding sagely, had probed into his past and dredged up items that had long since retired into the depths of his subconscious. In the end, this man had seemed rather disappointed to discover nothing in George's background which would account for this temporary slip into delinquency. He tutted a lot, shook his head a lot and made his report.

He told it to his commanding officer as he faced him, capless and flanked by two escorts. The CO had listened attentively, consulted the MO's and psychiatrist's reports, called witnesses (they had dragged in Jean who had stared at him coldly and told her story in a voice quivering with indignation) then proceeded to find him guilty of assault and conduct prejudicial to the good order of the Royal Air Force and sentenced him to 28 days detention.

And now he was back. Not to the solid, flesh-and-blood, 56 year-old George Reynolds, but to this shadowy counterpart – this *doppelgänger*, of indeterminate age, somehow caught up in a ghostly drama that had its origins 38 years ago. With that realisation, Dick Jenkins' face lost much of its reassuring quality. He became frightened. What was happening to him? There was a certain inexorable process at work over which he had no control and it terrified him. If he was a ghost like the others, why didn't he feel an affinity towards them? He was vastly relieved that he didn't have to look into those ghastly white eyes any more, but was at a loss to explain why they had suddenly assumed colour. Why did he appear to be getting younger? Was there some relationship between *that* and the involuntary occupation of his younger self – with such disastrous results? And what was the meaning of those fleeting visions and the bouts of excruciating pain that usually accompanied them? So many questions and no damned answers.

Now came the feeling of loneliness and isolation. He was marooned in a dimension to which he didn't belong – a castaway on a planet with a totally alien culture and environment. He shuddered and gave a groan of despair.

'I apologise for that somewhat abrupt halt, Mr Reynolds,' said Dick Jenkins, misinterpreting the groan for one of pain. 'You're not hurt are you?' His face still wore that anxious look.

George shook his head. 'Er . . . no, I don't think so.'

91

'You gave me quite a start, looking at me like that. I say,' a note of alarm crept into his voice. 'You're not about to leave us are you – return to your own time, I mean?'

George gave a mirthless laugh. 'I don't know. That seems to be something over which I have no control. But,' he added with a grimace, 'something happened to me just now, that's for sure.'

Dick Jenkins decided not to question George further. Explanations would take too long and, judging by George's appearance, time was beginning to run out. He let in the clutch, threw in the gear and trod on the accelerator. The tyres gave an initial screech of protest then settled down to a liquid muttering as the car shot down the road, paying no heed to the camp speed restrictions.

'Hang on just a little longer, Mr Reynolds, I want David Sheldon and his boys to see you and hear your story. Besides . . .' the note of alarm returned to his voice as a disturbing thought occurred to him, 'how the hell do I explain your disappearance? You're still technically under arrest you know.'

His foot pressed harder on the accelerator and the tyres protested furiously as the car turned into the expanse of tarmac in front of No. 1 hangar and onto the peritrack. Within seconds they were skidding to a halt in front of the pilot's crew room at No. 2 Dispersal.

# Chapter 11

The little convoy of vehicles drew up on the far side of the aircraft pen and immediately Dorothy, with the help of the others, began to offload the Range Rover. Plugs were inserted in their appropriate sockets, switches operated, generators hummed, scanners and direction finding aerials rotated, tape recorder spools span slowly and an oscilloscope sprang to life, the green line sweeping the screen in synchronisation with the scanner. A fast response temperature gauge and a barometric pressure gauge were sited strategically on the foundations of No. 2 Dispersal and, having satisfied herself that they worked, by blowing into them and intoning 'Testing, one, two three,' Dorothy set up two sensitive microphones, one at each end of the dispersal. She cast a final critical glance around the area, made a small adjustment to the voltage generator and then looked at her watch.

'In ten minutes, with any luck, we'll have laid these ghosts for good.'

Clive breathed deeply. 'I wish it were all over,' he said, fervently; 'with every passing minute my resolve weakens.'

'I know, Clive,' Dorothy gave his hand a sympathetic squeeze, 'but you wouldn't want to pull out now, would you? not when five years of training and preparation are just about to bear fruit.'

Clive sighed. 'No, I won't pull out, old girl. If only for my own peace of mind, I've got to see this thing through.'

'I say, will we be in any personal danger, Miss Beresford?' Peter Redford enquired anxiously.

Dorothy gazed out over the deceptively peaceful airfield. 'I don't know, Lord Redford. The behaviour of spirits at the moment of release is highly unpredictable. Some have been known to wreak vengeance on human beings for their enforced confinement; others go peacefully and gratefully. I'm hoping that these poor lost souls are of the latter category. 'However,' she grinned and pointed at the Revd Sinclair. 'There stands the best form of defence that I know of. Only very rarely will malignants attack a group which includes a man of God.' Her smile broadened 'Which makes one wonder whether there may not be something in this religion business after all. What do you say, my lord?'

'I have always been brought up to believe in God,' he answered, and added with a twinkle, 'but today I think I shall believe in Him just a little bit more.'

The ensuing laughter relieved the tension and the talk turned to more mundane topics until Dorothy looked at her watch.

'It's time,' she said quietly, 'are you ready Clive?'

He nodded. 'As ready as I'll ever be I guess.'

'Ye're a very brave man, wing commander,' the Revd Sinclair was moved to confess.

Clive gave him a wry smile. 'I think I'm a very foolish one, reverend.'

The man of God shrugged. 'That's as may be, but many foolhardy events have turned into acts of supreme bravery – take the charge of the light brigade, for instance.'

'But they paid a heavy price, remember.'

Ian Sinclair nodded in agreement. 'Aye, but they achieved their ultimate goal. God and my prayers go with you, Wing Commander.'

'Thank you, reverend.' Clive's smile was a little cynical. He was left with the distinct impression that the Revd Sinclair was only too ready to sacrifice him for the common cause.

'Oh, do come along, Clive,' Dorothy fretted, 'You know how essential it is that we get the timing right.'

He took her hand and she led him over the field to the dispersal site. They stopped in front of the right-hand concrete base.

'This is it, Dorothy, that one on the left was the ops room.'

'And where did you fall?'

Clive walked to a spot about six feet in front of, and central to, the base.

'Just about here.'

Dorothy nodded and once more, glanced at her watch. 'One minute, twenty five seconds to go.' She took both of Clive's hands and looked deep into his eyes. 'We've rehearsed this moment a hundred times, Clive, but there's one thing we couldn't rehearse and that is your course of action when you reach the other side. Over there, you're on your own. I have given you a few suggestions which will probably work under certain circumstances, but most of the time you'll be playing it by ear. It could be that you will possess certain powers over there making you a sort of superman; if so, use them sparingly and with care for they use up a great deal of energy. Now, remember I can only give you a maximum of ten minutes, then I'll have to bring you back. Remember, too, that we cannot equate the passage of time here with that over there, your ten minutes could be ten hours or even ten seconds. Try to keep note of the passage of time, Clive, I want to know how long it seemed to you that you were there. Now, my dear,' she tightened her grip on his hands, 'it is time – look into my eyes, look deeply, can you see the calmness there? There lies peace and serenity. You are relaxed, your eyes grow heavy, you are slipping into a deep, deep sleep.'

Clive's eyes snapped shut. Dorothy waited for a moment, then drew back her hand and delivered a stinging slap to his face. She gave a grunt of satisfaction at his lack of response, then kissed his reddened cheek. 'Take care, my dear,' she whispered, 'I love you'. She blinked and wiped away a couple of small tears that had forced their way unbidden from her eyes and ran slowly down her cheeks. She drew a deep breath and ran her fingers through her hair.

'It's 10.30 a.m. on Sunday September 15th 1940. Where are you now?'

'At the dispersal hut,' came the mechanical reply.

'What do you see?'

'I see this strange looking chap that Dick Jenkins has just brought in. I . . . I must be going mad – I can see straight through him. Says he's from the future. The others don't believe him – I do. He is trying to prove it by showing us a one-pound note. Says the head is that of Queen Elizabeth II, our princess.'

'That's the man, Clive. Remember, he's getting younger by the minute. It's imperative that he doesn't merge with his existing counterpart when their ages match. That age will be reached at 10.48. What do you see now?'

'A corporal has just poked his head through the door yelling "Scramble". Christ, why hadn't we been notified earlier? Everyone dives for the door. Skipper stops me and tells me to look after Chummie. Dick Jenkins is taking my place. He's beside himself with joy. Poor sod; hasn't flown since he was grounded for wrapping a Hurricane around a pylon while doing some illegal flying manoeuvres. Chummie's disappeared; run out of the hut. All hell's broken loose outside, bombs exploding everywhere. I can see a Stuka. It peels off and dives towards the airfield. Lord, that hideous scream. There go the bombs now. They've hit the cinema, oh my God, those poor sods inside. Hell, this is a massacre. There's an ME 109 machine-gunning the three Spits just about to lift off. I can see the flashes of the guns in the wings. The centre one is hit. It slews and smashes into the one on its right. There's a blinding flash. Now comes the sound of the explosion. Black smoke mushrooms out from the burning aircraft. The two aircraft, locked together, plough through the grass in a burning ball, hurling pieces of wreckage in all directions. They finally come to rest amid the splutter and crackle of exploding ammunition. One of those aircraft was mine.

I can see Chummie now, heading towards the aircraft pens, just ambling along as if he were out on a Sunday morning stroll. I start to run after him. There's a machine gun yammering away close by. Out of the corner of my eye, I can see these little spurts of dust erupting from the ground, they're . . .'

'Clive's eyes suddenly opened wide. His back arched, his mouth opened in a gurgling scream and his legs sagged. Dorothy struggled to support him, but his dead weight was too much for her and they both collapsed in a heap on the soft, dew-drenched grass.

# Chapter 12

The first thing George noticed as he stepped out of the car was the shadowy convoy he had seen entering the camp, parked haphazardly around the aircraft pen. The one with all the electronic gubbins was occupying the same piece of ground as the fuselage of a Mk. 2 Spitfire, while the Escort had its bonnet buried deeply into the tailplane. Figures like the one he had seen stepping through the cell door flitted fitfully around, seeming bent on some task or another. Before George could investigate further, he was grabbed by the arm and propelled into the crew room.

Five officer pilots occupied the room, but George's attention was immediately drawn to a young, good looking flying officer lounging nonchalantly against the bar. George blinked, rubbed his eyes and looked again. No, there was no mistaking it. While the appearance of the others was what George had become to accept as normal, this one was decidedly different. For one thing, he was transparent – not in the ordinary sense of the word as one sees through a sheet of solid glass, but rather as one views a mirage; it can be seen, and to all intents and purposes, it is there, but it's only an image and its reality lies elsewhere. He was accompanied by a second image, which was attached to him like a Siamese twin. This appendage was that of a much older man but so similar in appearance to its host, that it could have been his father or even himself in later years. Additionally, while the younger man was perfectly animated and behaved normally, his doppelgänger, although duplicating all his movements, had the appearance of a sleepwalker, the limbs moving woodenly, the eyes staring sightlessly ahead. The young officer, blissfully unaware of this wispy extension of

97

himself was giving George a reciprocal stare, his eyes wide in astonishment. Their eyes met momentarily and George looked away embarrassed, feeling somehow that he had witnessed some private act.

He was vaguely aware that he was speaking and, with a pang of alarm, he realised that he was beginning to lose touch again. Voices echoed hollowly around him; there was some ribald laughter which had the quality of tinkling bells, and a sound like a great wind filled the room. He experienced flashes of events long since forgotten as his probing spirit rapidly alternated between occupation and vacation of his younger self. It was as if, with the lesson of the recent abortive attempt well learned, it was tentatively testing the feasibility of a permanent transfer.

Someone was shouting and he was suddenly aware of a furious activity going on around him. He fought to contain his wandering spirit and was surprised to find that, if he concentrated hard enough on a particular object or event, he could satisfactorily control the frequency of these spirit transfusions. He remembered the ghostly convoy and the shadowy figures occupying No. 2 Dispersal, and decided to investigate.

He followed Dick Jenkins out of the hut and watched him run towards one of the parked aircraft. It was only then that he became aware that a raid was in progress. He heard the roar of the aircraft, the scream of falling bombs and felt the force of their subsequent detonations; saw the two Spitfires pile up and heard the rattle of machine guns and saw the bullets spattering the ground unpleasantly close behind him. He heard a cry and swung round to see the young flying officer fall to the ground, a rapidly widening crimson stain spreading over his tunic.

Instinctively, he turned and ran to his aid, but came to an abrupt halt at the sight of the injured man's *doppelgänger*, now completely opaque, detach itself from the body and rise to its feet. For a moment, it gazed down at its former host and then looked around, taking in every detail of its surroundings.

'We made it, Dorothy, by God, we made it. Sweetheart, you're a bloody marvel.'

Clive's eyes finally came to rest on George. They were pupil-less and black as the darkest night, yet there was life there. They were warm and moist which gave them added lustre, glistening as they moved, while deep in their unfathomable depths, there was a translucent glow which shimmered, constantly changing colour and shape.

Try as he might, George was unable to tear his gaze away from those fascinating eyes; he was powerless to move, his muscles refusing to obey the frantic commands issuing from his brain. The sounds of battle receded and a silence, heavy and oppressive, enveloped him. His surroundings grew blurred and indistinct, only the doppelgänger remained in focus. Then it spoke.

At first George had difficulty making out the words. They had an indefinable quality which seemed to clang and echo inside his head, like the clamour of bells reverberating around the walls of a belfry. This effect didn't last long, however, and George was pleased to find that, when the words grew distinct, they carried a pleasant, mellow quality.

'So you're the guy who's been causing all the trouble. I take it you *are* George Reynolds?'

Dumbly, George nodded his head, wondering at the same time how it was that this apparition came to know his name; and what was all this 'trouble' he was being accused of causing?

Clive gave a satisfactory nod. 'Good. Allow me to introduce myself. I am Clive Prescott, the future version of the unfortunate fellow you see lying here.'

George suddenly found his voice. 'Christ, I'm going mad. What the hell am I doing in this Godforsaken place? Stop looking at me like that. Oh God, what is happening to me?' The last, a piteous cry from the heart.

For an instant, Clive's face softened. His eyes lost their black, hypnotic quality and grew warm and blue. George, finding himself free of his mesmeric bonds, turned and fled. Sight and sound returned and he ran, not caring where, as long as it was away from those compelling eyes.

A figure suddenly materialised directly in his path and he ran headlong into Clive's outstretched arms. There was a short, brief struggle but George was too shocked to put up much resistance and soon found himself held tightly by the shoulders. Despite his reluctance to do so, his eyes were drawn to the other's face. To his relief, the face seemed normal. It was that of a man, perhaps the same age as himself, still handsome with a clipped moustache and humorous, kindly eyes. Despite himself, George felt drawn towards this fellow and lost a lot of his fear.

'How . . . how did you do that?' he gasped.

Clive looked just as bewildered as George. 'Dunno, really.' Then he grinned. 'I'm new to this sort of thing. I just thought myself in this position and, *voila!* There I was.'

'But what do you want with me?' asked George plaintively, 'and how do you know my name?'

'Believe me, son (this in deference to George's youthful appearance) 'I know a great deal about you. To put it mildly, you're a bloody menace.'

George bristled. 'Me, a bloody menace. What do you mean by that? What have I ever done to you?'

'It's not so much what you've done to me, it's what you've done to all those poor lost souls you've kept earthbound for the past 38 years, and I'm here to try and get things back on course. This I intend to do – one way or another,' he added grimly.

The last bomb of the raid fell close by, causing both men to duck instinctively and the last of the raiders, a Junkers 87, banked sharply and headed south, its pulsating drone growing gradually weaker, until eventually silenced by distance. Clive and George grimly viewed the appalling carnage that surrounded them.

A thick pall of black smoke rose from the shattered station, obscuring the sun, and slowly drifted east. Bomb craters pitted the airfield and roadways, making it impossible for the depleted fire-fighting team to reach any but the nearest buildings. The hangars, now gaunt skeletal structures of twisted girders and rubble, formed a massive funeral pyre for the aircraft and tradesmen that once worked in them. A few yards away, on the peritrack, a bowser teetered on the edge of a bomb crater which had suddenly erupted in front of it. Its driver lay half in and half out of the open door. Miraculously it had not exploded, but gallons of high octane fuel poured out of a jagged hole in the tank, flooding the road and seeping over the edge of the crater where it formed an ever-increasing pool, awaiting that single spark which would trigger off a holocaust. Bodies lay scattered around, their grotesque positions reflecting the agony of their death throes, and the air reeked with the acrid smell of smoke and petrol fumes. A shattering explosion rent the air and a pall of smoke blossomed up from the bomb dump where a stack of 1000 lb high explosive bombs had sympathetically detonated.

With these scenes of carnage burned indelibly into his brain, George rounded on Clive. 'How can you say that I'm responsible for all this . . . this?' Words failed him and he flapped his arms hopelessly.

'I didn't say that you were responsible for it,' Clive said, slowly, 'I said that you were responsible for perpetuating it.'

'But I don't understand,' said George, miserably. His eyes scanned Clive's face beseechingly. 'I don't know what I am or why I'm here. Please help me, I'll do anything you say, anything.' George's shoulders sagged and he looked the picture of dejection.

Clive smiled and put a friendly arm around George's shoulders, turning him until he faced the concrete dispersal.

'Tell me,' he said pointing, 'what do you see there?'

George shook his head. 'No, you'd think I was mad.'

'Then let me tell you what you see. You see three vehicles and four figures. You don't see them distinctly, they're all sort of fuzzy and hazy. You can't make out their faces and they flit about so that one moment they're there and the next somewhere else. Perhaps one of them lies immobile. Can you see him?'

George nodded, his eyes fixed hypnotically on the misty scene before him. 'I think so.'

'Well, believe it or not, that's me,' said Clive, who had difficulty believing it himself.

George tore his eyes from the scene. 'You?' He laughed humourlessly. 'Two of you, I can believe,' nodding at the inert figure of the young flying officer, 'I saw it with my own eyes, but three of you takes a bit of swallowing.'

'Nevertheless,' said Clive simply, 'swallow it you must.' George felt his patience draining rapidly away. 'For God's sake, man, come to the point. Who are those figures, why are you here and, for that matter, what the hell am I doing here?'

After the unnatural silence which followed the raid, the station was beginning to show signs of life. Voices, attenuated with distance could be heard calling to each other. Somewhere, in the dog compound, a dog barked and was immediately taken up by its companions with a chorus of yelps and howls. A car suddenly appeared from behind the ruins of a hangar, dodging the rubble and weaving around the bomb craters, and then made off in the direction of the bomb dump. Life, or what was left of it, was beginning to return to RAF Lynton Down.

Clive peered into the middle distance, gave a perplexed shake of the head, and then looked at George.

'Strange, you being able to see them, but then, Dorothy said you might, clever girl. Those people, George, strange as it may seem, are about the only real things around here. They, or at least one of them, is responsible for me being here.'

George was still trying to cope with the idea of there being three Clives and Clive smiled at his woebegone expression.

'I can see that I shall have to put you in the picture, but we haven't much time, so I'll make it brief.'

'Well, hallelujah for that,' muttered George.

Clive grinned. 'By now, you will have realised that you are trapped in a time zone centred on a doomed RAF station, in the year 1940. Ever since you arrived here, you have been associating with people who died in the raid you have just witnessed. Most of them lie in a mass grave in the village churchyard.'

George shook his head. 'Not all. I've seen one who I know for a fact was not killed in the raid, and then there's yourself, you survived.'

'Obviously there were survivors,' said Clive, impatiently, 'but only a few of them are alive today and those would have been totally invisible to you.'

'I saw you, although you were sort of transparent and accompanied by an appendage, an older version of yourself.'

Clive's eyebrows rose in surprise. 'The devil you say. Mm, I guess our timing must have been a little out. I must remember to tell Dorothy when I get back. I remember, though, the shock of seeing you for the first time. I could see right through you, too.'

'Who's this Dorothy you keep mentioning?' asked George. 'Is she the one who sent you here?'

'Yes. She's a member of the Institute of Psychic Research and has been studying this case for the past five years. She's a girl in a million and, do you know, I think I've fallen in love with her.' He chuckled. 'Fancy that, and at my age, too.' He lapsed into a brooding silence, no doubt mulling over the chances of his love being reciprocated. Then he sighed. 'But I digress. You're not dead, you realise that don't you?'

George felt a moment of elation. He wasn't dead, oh, thank God. All along he had felt different from the others. There was that initial ghastly whiteness of their eyes, and he was the only one who had been getting younger. At that thought, his spirit, which had recently been so admirably restrained, again took flight. This time, it lingered awhile, perhaps uncertain whether this was the right moment for permanent transfer, and George had time to look about him.

He was sitting in the rear turret of a Wellington bomber, his eyes focused on a thin aiming cross, his right hand operating the controls to manoeuvre the sight into alignment with a target set up 100 feet away in sandbanked butts enclosed on three sides by a high brick wall. The four .303 Browning machine guns had recently been harmonised and now they were going to be fired in a proving exercise.

The turret tracked to the left with the guns elevating, until the crosses of sight and target superimposed. Holding the turret in that position, George briefly thumbed the firing button. The guns hammered out a short burst and stopped. George watched the bullets kick up four separate spurts of sand behind the target and imagined that they were tearing their way through the vital parts of an enemy aircraft. In fact, he could see it quite clearly. Trailing a long streamer of black smoke, the black HE one eleven slipped to port and began a long, shallow dive earthward. He depressed the guns and loosed off another burst into the stricken aircraft. It went into a roll, its angle deepening. The roll became a spiral and one, two, three, four small figures detached themselves from the doomed aircraft, falling with it for a short distance until brought up abruptly by the blossoming parachutes.

George's teeth bared in a savage snarl as he trained his guns on the helpless figures. His thumb whitened on the firing button . . .

'Come back, come back.' A voice, tiny at first and far away, swiftly became a booming unbearable sound, filled with a sense of urgency. George opened his eyes and stared at Clive uncomprehendingly.

'Come back.' The voice had assumed a normal quality, but the sense of urgency was still there. This was followed by a stinging slap on George's left cheek and then his whole body was shaken violently.

'Come back you bastard. I'm not going to lose you now.'

Slowly comprehension returned. He shook his head and raised his arm to ward of another blow to the cheek.

'Alright, alright,' he shouted, 'I'm back.'

Clive's arm dropped to his side and he let out a long-drawn-out sigh of relief.

'Thank Christ for that.' He gripped George's shoulders as if he would retain the spirit by imprisoning the body and looked deep into his eyes.

'Now, listen to me,' he snapped, 'I have the power to destroy both you and that wandering spirit of yours and just to prove it, here's a little sample.'

George's eyes suddenly opened wide as a huge jolt contracted every muscle in his body. A blue glow surrounded him, his chest tightened and his lungs refused to expand. He began to enter the first stages of suffocation.

Then the steel bands that clamped his chest snapped open and he was free. He sucked in life-giving lungfuls of air until his heart ceased to hammer and his breathing returned to normal.

'For God's sake don't do that again,' George gasped, 'you've proved your point.' His brow creased in a puzzled frown. 'One thing I'd like to know, though, how is it that I retain all the human sensations? If I'm a ghost or whatever, why do I still feel the necessity to breathe? I can even feel the beat of my heart.'

Clive nodded. 'I remember Dorothy saying once, during one of our sessions, "Of course he will still have a lot of his earthly attributes." She likened it to a person with a severed limb. They still feel that it is there, can wiggle their toes and want to scratch the foot when it itches. Your body still lives, therefore you experience earthly sensations.'

'I see,' George said slowly, 'now I know the reason why I experienced those dreadful visions. I was actually seeing and feeling everything my body felt during its brief moments of consciousness.' Another thought occurred to him. 'And when their eyes reverted to their natural colour, I was as near death as makes no difference?'

'Exactly,' Clive smiled, 'and you still are, have no doubt about that. What we must do now is to stop you taking over your younger self. It couldn't be done before because we had to wait for the actual date of your accident.' His voice grew serious. 'This is our one and only chance to end the cycle and lay these poor souls to rest. To do that, you must return to the body you left at the scene of the accident. If I fail, you and all those other souls will never know peace. You and they will relieve the horrors of this day for all eternity. Do you know what that means? Can you imagine eternity, George? Not only that,' Clive added grimly, 'having reached the point of no return, the others have now become malignant and any contact between them and a living creature would mean instant death for the latter. So you see how imperative it is that, with my help, you return to your own body and not to that of your younger self, whose age, by the way, you are rapidly approaching.'

'I see,' said George, thoughtfully. It would be nice to be young again, to relive his life, which on the whole, had been a happy one. But for the cycle to repeat itself for all eternity! He shuddered at the thought. And what about the living; his wife and children. He worshipped Laura and she him. He couldn't die now, there was still so much to be done. Above all, he wanted to grow old with her, to complete their remaining years in the love and companionship that had always been a part of their married life. He wanted to feel, once more, the soft, small arms of his grandchildren around his neck and to hear them say, 'I love my Grandad.' George choked down a lump in his throat and clutched desperately at Clive's arm.

'For God's sake get me out of here, Clive. I want to go home.'

Clive breathed an inaudible sigh of relief. His task would prove much easier with George's co-operation. He patted George's shoulder. 'And go home you shall, my friend,' he said quietly.

'But please, hurry,' said George in a fit of agitation. 'This compulsion to return to my younger self grows stronger by the moment, and I don't know whether I shall have the strength to fight it.'

'I'll give you that strength,' Clive reassured him. 'Just hang on to that determination to go home. Now, look into my eyes.'

With a certain amount of misgiving, George did as he was bidden. Clive's eyes stared back at him, piercing, probing, penetrating the very depths of his soul. The eyes disappeared and, in their place, a swirling blue-grey mist filled the empty sockets which deepened and darkened until he could imagine he was gazing into twin whirlpools of inky blackness and unfathomable depth. Slowly, they merged and became one vast maelstrom into which he found he was being inexorably drawn.

A blackness, deep and complete, encompassed him. Although there were no reference points, he sensed that he was moving as if pulled by invisible strings. Suddenly, some distance away, a faint glow appeared. As he drew near he saw, to his horror, that it was a disembodied head floating and bobbing gently in the darkness. Behind it, other heads began to appear until there was a line of them stretching into an indeterminate distance and shedding an eerie blue glow in the otherwise total blackness.

George was close enough now to the first head to plainly see its features and, with a shock, he recognised the scarred face of Dick Jenkins. It was a death's-head, the ghastly white skin stretched tightly over the skull, the thin lips drawn back over clenched teeth, the eyes closed and sunk in deep hollows.

He wanted to scream, but no sound came forth. Every nerve and fibre in his body strained against the force that carried him forward, but to no avail. As he drew level with the head, the eyes slowly opened and fixed George with a baleful glare. Then, as if it recognised in George a friend, the eyes grew warm, round and pleading, colour returned to the cheeks and the lips filled and closed in repose. The mouth opened and it spoke.

'Help us, help us to die.'

The voice was breathless, harsh and mechanical and it kept repeating its plea over and over again, rising in desperation as the distance between them increased.

Other heads, too, were recognisable as those belonging to the people who had died in the raid, and each responded in a like fashion to the first.

'Help us. Help us to die.'

As the sound of each voice faded, another took its place until George's brain reeled under the hammer blow of each word. He shut his eyes and blocked his ears against the nightmarish visions and that haunting phrase, but the images invaded his mind, the words still burnt their way deep into his subconcious.

Then, as if someone had switched off an over-loud radio, the sights and sounds abruptly ceased. Silence, so oppressive that it could almost be felt, descended upon him like heavy curtain folds. He experienced a deep calmness and tranquillity of mind which, like some opiate, numbed his senses and bade him deliver himself to the peace and serenity of total oblivion. He sighed as a tired man sighs when he snuggles down to sleep after the day's labours.

A small sound, gradually growing louder and more persistent, penetrated his clouded brain. He frowned and tried to ignore it, but it wouldn't go away. Irritably, George gave it his full attention.

At first he had difficulty in identifying it, but it soon became apparent that the sounds were the soft, muted, sobs of a woman crying as if her heart would break. With a tremendous effort, he opened his eyes and gazed upon familiar surroundings. He was at home, in his own sitting room, and there, sitting in her favourite chair, was his wife, Laura, her tear-stained face staring sightlessly ahead, her shoulders heaving with uncontrollable sobs. Instinctively George knew the reason for her sorrow and knelt in front of her.

'Laura, dear heart, don't cry. I'm not dead. See, I'm here, dearest.'

He stretched out his hand to raise her chin, to make her look at him, but found that he couldn't touch her. His hand stopped an inch or so from her face and, try as he might, he could force it no further. It was as if she were surrounded by an invisible, unassailable barrier.

Almost weeping with frustration, he stood up and gazed down upon her. Never, until this moment, had he realised how much he loved her, how much he had become dependent upon her. She was more than his life. Without her by his side, he was an empty shell, bereft of its living component.

Laura sighed, wiped her eyes with her tear-soaked handkerchief and stood up. Helpless to do anything but watch, George's eyes followed her as she walked slowly to the mantelpiece. Her hand moved towards his pipe rack and her fingers gently caressed each pipe. She turned, walked over to the piano and picked up a framed picture of himself and Laura taken on a holiday in Malta some years previously. Two laughing, sun-tanned faces, framed by the fronds of a stubby palm tree, stared back at her – a moment of happiness frozen by the camera. Her lips trembled and tears sprang afresh in her eyes. Clasping the picture to her heart, she ran from the room. He listened to the sound of her footsteps on the stairs and creak of springs as she flung herself upon the bed.

He gazed around the room; at the well loved, familiar objects; pictured himself, comfortably seated before a cheery fire, his pipe clamped between his teeth, watching with affection, his wife, knitting needles click-clacking away, patiently knitting some knick-knack or other for the grandchildren. Hot tears sprang to his eyes and a terrible rage welled up inside him, all his anger directed at Clive for subjecting him to this anguish.

'You bastard,' he ground out between clenched teeth, 'I'll kill you for this. Bring me back, you devil, BRING ME BACK.' The last words were yelled with all the force of his lungs.

He was still shouting it, when Clive closed his eyes and released George from the spell. It took a moment or two for him to realise that he was back, then he sprang at Clive with a howl of rage. The next instant, he was flat on his back, hurled there by some tremendous force. Breathless and dazed, he was vaguely aware that Clive was speaking.

'Sorry about that, old chap, didn't mean to use so much force. Haven't quite got the hang of these new powers yet.' He grinned and helped George to his feet. 'Now, listen to me. It was necessary to put you through that terrible experience for two reasons. One, to concentrate your mind and prevent your permanent emergence with your younger self; and two, to show you a little of the sadness and anguish which your death would bring about. I have achieved the first object, it is now past the point where your ages coincide and any further attempted transference by you would be dangerous, if not impossible. You now have two courses open to you. You can remain suspended in eternal limbo, remembering that you may never again return to your youth, that link has been broken; or you can return to the body you left at the scene of the accident and give it life.'

He paused for a moment and cocked his head to one side, listening. A voice, Dorothy's voice, tiny and filled with a sense of urgency was forming words inside his head.

'Is it done, Clive? I must bring you back soon.'

Clive closed his eyes and concentrated. 'A few more minutes, Dorothy, give me just a few more minutes.'

His response to Dorothy's voice was instinctive and he had no means of knowing whether she had received his message, so his next words to George reflected some of her urgency.

'Now, quickly man, make up your mind, I haven't much time left.'

'Then get me back. Please don't leave me now. Tell me what I have to do.' Desperation forced the words from George's throat in a rush.

'Hold my hands and trust me.'

George grasped his hands eagerly. There was a sharp pop,

like a bursting balloon and, beginning in September 1940, George's life flashed past his eyes. He felt himself caught up in it – a part of it, but no actual moment lingered long enough to savour the nostalgic sweetness. The years passed as seconds, each attenuated event crammed into a thousandth part of it. Then, at first imperceptibly, he noticed that time was slowing down. The years lengthened. He would linger long enough in one to recognise certain events, and even be able to put a date to them. The months became distinguishable one from the other and then the weeks. Soon the days passed as seconds until, on the day of the fateful accident, he was viewing his life at a normal pace. He relived the squadron reunion and his journey home right up to the moment when he narrowly missed the lorry and failed to take the corner. The balloon popped again. He was floating gently above a hospital bed, gazing down on himself. His head was heavily bandaged and one arm, bound in splints, was supported by a rope. An oxygen mask was clamped over his nose and a bottle, suspended above the bed, fed small drips of liquid down a plastic tube and into his arm. Wires attached to vital parts of his body were fed out to various electronic apparatus which recorded his heartbeat, breathing and blood pressure.

As George looked down on himself, a great sense of peace overwhelmed him. He felt himself drawn towards his body on the bed. He was tired, but it was a pleasant lassitude. Soon he would see Laura again. With a profound sigh of contentment, he merged and the returning spirit rekindled the almost extinguished flame of life. George Reynolds stirred and groaned. The nurse glanced up sharply from her magazine.

# Chapter 13

A t that precise moment, on an exposed and windswept part of the old airfield, Dorothy Beresford looked at her watch for the hundredth time and gazed down on the prone figure of Clive Prescott.

'Should ye no' be bringing him back, lassie?' the Revd Sinclair ventured, tentatively.

Dorothy hesitated in an agony of indecision. Was the job done? She had no way of knowing. Had she only imagined that Clive had asked for a few more minutes? Since then there had been no further message from him. If she brought him back now, before he had time to complete his work, all those years of preparation would go for nothing. On the other hand, if she delayed, even for another few seconds, it might prove fatal. Clive was strong and in good condition, but she was treading new ground and who knows how long the body can sustain life when the spirit has been released in a state of cataclysmic shock? As far as she knew, George Reynolds still lived, but in Clive's case, the circumstances were somewhat different. His spirit had been released by the hypnotically induced reality of the shock of a bullet fired 38 years ago, whereas George Reynolds' spirit was involuntarily released from a body, mangled and close to death, in an accident that had occurred only a few hours ago. She couldn't – wouldn't – risk it. She bent over and kissed Clive's cheek, then her mouth moved close to his ear.

'Clive, my dear,' she whispered, 'I must bring you back. If the job is not done, forget it. Now listen; you hear only my voice. I'm going to count to three and give you a small electric shock. When you feel the charge, you will awake.' As she spoke she was hurriedly unbuttoning his shirt to bare his chest.

'Lord Redford, pass me those electrodes. Quickly man,' she snapped as he showed signs of tardiness.

She placed the electrodes on either side of his chest and began to count. 'One, two, three.' She pressed a button and Clive's body gave an involuntary jump. Immediately, he opened his eyes. For a moment, he seemed to have difficulty in focusing them; then he grinned and winked at Dorothy.

'We did it old girl, by golly we did it. I've said it before, and I'll say it again, you're a ruddy marvel.' He grasped her face with both hands and kissed her soundly on the mouth.

'That will be enough of that, Clive Prescott.' Dorothy stood up and smoothed her hair and clothes to hide her confusion. Her voice was indignant, but the flush of pleasure on her cheeks belied the tone.

Clive, too, scrambled to his feet and put his arm around Dorothy's waist. They both gazed out over the flat expanse of the old airfield, with its hangars and derelict buildings in the background, seeing it again as it was in its prime, and listening to the faraway echoes of the roar of aircraft engines, the clamour and bustle of a station at war and, above all, the laughter and tears of the people who had lived and died within its precincts. Slowly, the echoes died away, leaving only the song of a meadow lark and the soft rustle of the wind in the grass to break the silence.

Dorothy gave a contented sigh. 'Your ghosts are laid, Lord Redford,' she said softly. 'RAF Lynton Down is at peace.'